CALL OF THE NIGHT SINGERS

RACHEL LANGELLA

CONTENTS

CHAPTER 1

I shall never forget my first sight of Heatherford House, even though I have often wished I could purge the memory from my mind, the way one desires to forget all reminders of nightmares. At the time, I had not the slightest inkling of the depths of depravity I would discover hidden within its dank and weathered facade, and I thought it merely a crumbling ruin better suited for demolition than habitation.

Even though the house is central to the occurrences I shall set forth, it is not the beginning of my tale. As with most momentous events in life, I had no foreshadowing that my mundane existence would be impacted so profoundly by the simple act of giving a poetry reading.

As a young man of some small means and few practical skills, I had chosen to attain a degree in Classics from the College of Charleston, a fact which did little to endear me to my father, who wished me to follow along in his footsteps in the family business. But I was far more interested in books than in ships, even though my father had worked hard to rebuild the Oceanic Transport Company from the ruins left to him by his family after the War Between the States. Fortunately, my younger brother heard the call of the sea, and so I was free to pursue my interest in Greek and Latin, especially in the form of poetry and drama, which led me to become Professor Geoffrey Wainwright, and I acquired a position on the faculty of Blount College, a venerable institution located in the beautiful Piedmont area of North Carolina. My position was why I was giving a poetry reading at one of the cultural events jointly sponsored by my own department and the Department of Philosophy.

I chose to read an elegy by Alexander Aetolus, a rather obscure writer, although one whose work was recognized as being quite beautiful. I read the poem first in Greek, then recited a lyrical translation of my own, dwelling on the elegance and perfection of the passage in which the subject of the poem, Antheus,

Stood in awe of Zeus,
Of the libations he had held at Phobius' house
And of the salt of hospitality,
Which will wash away the unseemly word in seas,
springs, and rivers

My modest effort was well received, and I accepted several handshakes and murmurs of approbation from my fellow faculty members. I was, of course, quite pleased by this response, although public performance has never been among my favorite activities. I was relieved when the next performer, a student pianist, earnestly applied herself to the keyboard to render a Chopin nocturne with some eloquence. I repaired to the refreshment table and gratefully accepted a glass of champagne punch from the attendant.

A man who looked to be about my own age approached the table; however, he seemed more interested in me than in the punch. "That was beautifully done," he said, offering a sweet and open smile. "I was quite transported."

I would be remiss not to mention that I had departed even further from my family's approval when it came to the preferred subjects of my attraction as well as my preferred career. While the young woman at the piano was considered lovely by the standards of society, she did not captivate me in face or form the way this young man did. I was taller, and he was of slender build. The elegant figure he presented in his evening suit made my breath catch. His hair was the color of golden honey, and its appearance of softness made me long to run my fingers through it. But it was his eyes that reached within me and ensnared my very soul. They were as wide and guileless as a child's and as blue as the Carolina summer sky. I could not speak, and I feared he would think me witless.

"Thank you," I said at last, although my voice was husky and far more breathless than during my reading. I extended my hand. "I have not had the pleasure of making your acquaintance, sir."

"Garland Heatherford of Philosophy." Garland stretched out his white gloved hand and clasped mine, and I saw a flash of understanding in his eyes as he peeked at me from beneath his lashes. "A pleasure, sir."

I felt the warmth of his fingers even through our gloves, and a pleasurable tingle flowed over me. "Indeed, the pleasure is mine, Mr. Heatherford. I take it you are a fan of the classics?"

"I am, although perhaps more so after your reading." Garland's voice sounded as husky as my own. "You are quite a masterful speaker."

"You flatter me." I tightened my fingers on his before releasing his hand with reluctance to avoid attracting undue attention from our fellows. I found, however, I wanted far more of *Garland's* attention. "Any time you wish me to read for you, I am at your service."

Garland's expressive eyes widened briefly, and then he nodded. "Perhaps we could arrange a private reading one evening? I would enjoy hearing more of your translations."

Garland's words convinced me that we had more in common than a fondness for poetry. Indeed, my conviction was proven in less than a month, when an evening of reading and several glasses of sherry resulted in a meeting of lips as well as of minds. I took Garland to my bed, finding his pale, slender body and silken skin far more worthy of my attention than poets who had long since turned to dust.

Even though I was not yet thirty, I knew with certainty Garland and I were destined for one another, a feeling he shared; he greeted my suggestion that we exchange our separate rooming houses for a home of our own with unbridled enthusiasm. The arrangement was as much pragmatic as romantic, however, as having a place of our own, away from prying eyes, helped to keep us safe from the gossips and scandalmongers who seem, like hideous insects, to wait in corners to spring upon the unwary. Thus, we were able, over the course of four years, to develop similar reputations as academics far too engrossed in work to care about keeping company with the fairer sex, and we were careful to maintain some separate friendships with our colleagues so people would not categorize us as a couple.

As the century neared its end, I was the most content of men. I had a job I enjoyed, a small but tasteful home containing all those mundane comforts a man considers necessary and, most importantly, a partner who shared my tastes and suited me in all ways, both in and out of bed. I was, quite simply, a man in love and at peace with life, desiring nothing more than what Fate had gifted me, save that nothing stripped from me any part of my existence.

As the summer of 1899 began, Garland and I decided we had earned a sabbatical to travel to those places about which we'd both read but had neither the means nor the opportunity to visit. We both applied for and received a semester off from our teaching duties for "enrichment and education," and thus we made plans to travel to Greece in the fall, with a mind toward making side trips to Egypt and parts of the Middle East as time and money permitted. Many pleasant evenings were spent in discussion and contemplation of our itinerary, with Garland as eager as I for the opportunity to share in the joys of travel and discovery.

But Garland received a letter at the beginning of September that brought our plans to a sudden and unpleasant halt. I knew Garland's moods and expressions too well not to recognize at once that he was troubled when he opened it. His brow furrowed as he read the letter, and the light in his eyes was dimmed.

"I feel rather like Hamlet." He leaned forward in his chair and offered me the letter. We were seated by the fireplace, cups of tea at hand and our chairs facing each other for convenience if we wished to converse. "This letter bears mirth in a funeral and a dirge in marriage, in a way. My cousin Orry is dead, and now I am named the heir of my great-uncle Roderick's fortune."

I accepted the sheet of paper and scanned it. The document spelled out the staggering sum of the inheritance as well as the command that Garland must appear no later than the first of October in order to sign certain documents to formalize his status.

"Is this in earnest?" I glanced at Garland, letting him see my shock. "You never mentioned having Croesus in your family tree!"

"I'd no idea I might inherit." Garland spread his hands and shrugged. "Orry was a man in his prime, and I had every expectation that he might live to inherit where the others before him had not. Unfortunately, he was taken by consumption, and now the whole lot falls to me."

Surprisingly, he did not appear at all pleased by the prospect of inheriting more wealth than I could imagine. I put the letter aside and leaned forward to take Garland's hands in mine. His fingers were long, slender, and elegant, and I caressed them gently in the way he liked best.

"Is it the macabre manner of becoming heir, or is there something else about this legacy which troubles you?"

Garland tightened his fingers around mine, worry blooming in the depths of his gaze. "I have too many questions regarding the fates of the previous heirs. I find it odd they have all met untimely ends at a young age while my uncle lives on."

I felt a chill. Garland was the most cheerful of men, full of curiosity and eagerness to experience new things. I'd never seen him like this before, his blue eyes dark and pensive, the smile gone from his face as though it might never return.

"How many heirs have there been? If your great-uncle has lived a long life, perhaps they simply met with ill luck."

"My uncle has reached his eightieth year." Garland turned his gaze to the small Aubusson rug between our chairs and rubbed the back of my hand with his thumb. "There have been five heirs before me. I will be the sixth, but if their ill luck befalls me, I may not be the last. Of the five, only Orry's death seems natural. Nothing has ever been said of the others, of course, because my uncle is a rich and powerful man, but I cannot be the only one who questions how four other men all happened to drown after becoming his heir."

"Four men drowned?"

I had to admit that having five other heirs meeting an untimely death might make the prospect of inheriting seem less attractive, yet there had to be an explanation. I am not the most adventurous of men, but even I thought Garland might be a touch paranoid.

"It seems as though you have two choices: to accept or to decline the offer," I said, gripping his hands. "But if you are correct, someone else would be put in danger."

Garland shook his head, as I knew he might. "I could not allow someone to come to harm because of unmanly cowardice. If, however, my suspicions are wrong, and their deaths were nothing more than tragic accidents...." He smiled wryly, a flash of self-deprecation in his eyes.

"Then someday I will be a very rich man indeed, and you and I will be able to travel as we please."

"The money is not important. You are." I fixed him with a solemn gaze. "But remember you have one thing the previous heirs did not: me. Whither thou goest, as the saying goes."

I would do anything to keep Garland safe. If he decided to accept his uncle's offer, I would accompany him to sign the documents. I could not imagine what harm a man in his eighties could do to one man in his thirties, but there was safety in numbers.

Garland's smile softened into warm affection, and he lifted my hand to his lips and pressed a kiss to the back of it. "I need fear nothing with you by my side, Geoffrey. Very well, then. I will write to accept, and we will travel to Bath to meet my uncle. I have never seen Heatherford House, and my parents spoke little of Uncle Roderick, so I've no idea what to expect."

"Let us hope he is an entertaining host, since we are giving up Greece for his benefit." I was not a student of law, so I was uncertain what documents Garland was required to sign. Frankly, I wondered if the demand for Garland's presence was nothing more than a manipulative or lonely old man's theatrics, but I did not voice my suspicions. It would be unfair of me to prejudice him further against his uncle, especially since Garland's own doubts seemed great enough as it was. "You write to your uncle, and I shall write to cancel our trip."

Garland sighed as he released my hands and leaned back in his chair. "I regret the loss. I was looking forward to surveying the ruins of the Delphi theatre and the Parthenon and marveling over the beauty of that lost age with you. We will go," he added with a look of fierce determination. "When this business with my uncle is settled, we will make our plans anew."

"Of course we shall," I said.

A sense of foreboding passed through me even as I said the words, but not being a man given to flights of fancy, I dismissed it as merely disappointment and set about changing our travel plans with alacrity.

CHAPTER 2

Bath was the oldest town in North Carolina, but despite its historical importance, it had failed to prosper. It was little more than a large village located on the banks of the Pamlico River. A local legend claimed the town had been chastised in 1762 for its "deadly sins" by none other than George Whitefield, a Methodist evangelist who was considered the personification of the Great Awakening. Disgusted by the residents' disrespectful response to his preaching, Whitefield took off his shoes and shook them to remove the dust of the town, and in doing so, he laid a curse upon the town: "I say to the village of Bath, village you shall remain, now and forever, forgotten by men and nations until such time as it pleases God to turn the light of His countenance again upon you."

As a modern man, I put no stock in curses, but I couldn't deny that Bath was a backwater town in many ways, including available modes of transportation. To reach our destination, we were obliged to travel from

Charlotte to Raleigh via one rail line, then change to another to continue on from Raleigh to the little town of Washington. There we left modern conveyances behind us and switched to a carriage which carried both passengers and mail further east, parallel to the river.

We finally reached Bath in the late afternoon, some three days before Garland's deadline. There was no livery stable where we could acquire horses to carry us to our destination, so after asking directions at the coach house, we picked up our bags and began a rather long walk along the dusty track which led from Bath down toward the banks of the Pamlico.

Garland's unease seemed to grow as we drew closer to Heatherford House. Although he made no outward complaint, his face grew pale, which one might ascribe to the unaccustomed exertion, but I knew him well enough to see the lines of worry deepening on his features. He was no happier about being Roderick's heir now than he had been when we first received the news.

I attempted to lighten the mood by calling his attention to the songs of the bright crimson cardinals flitting in the trees and the colorful pansies lining our path, but Garland was too preoccupied with his own thoughts to listen. I lapsed into silence, fervently hoping the reception we received at the end of our journey would alleviate Garland's fears and restore my lover to his normally sunny disposition.

Unfortunately, the sight greeting our eyes in the fading autumn twilight was not one designed to lift the heart of the weary traveler. The path turned abruptly at a high hedgerow, which was ragged and interspersed with weeds and half-grown trees. We followed this to an opening, where a large iron gate hung askew on broken, rusted hinges. I didn't see how such a portal could lead to a residence where a man of Garland's uncle's wealth resided, but a brass plaque on the gate indicated we had reached Heatherford House.

I smiled at Garland despite my own trepidation. "He probably doesn't look outside often," I said, keeping my tone light.

Garland shuddered, and his expressive eyes filled with dread as he gazed at the dilapidated gate and the section of the desolate house beyond it. "Must we go inside? I know we've come all this way, but now I wish we had not."

I put down my bag and placed my hands on Garland's shoulders. "If you like, we will turn around and depart this very moment. But ask yourself if that is what you truly wish, love, and if your reasons for coming in the first place have changed at all."

Garland tore his gaze away from the gate, and his features grew firm with resolve. "No, I still intend to spare anyone else from suffering the fate of my predecessors. Perhaps you and I will break the curse together and there will be no more drownings."

"I have no intention of drowning nor of allowing you to do so either. The sooner you sign those papers, the sooner we can leave this place and return to our own home." I smiled and squeezed Garland's shoulders. "I have no desire to share your good company with anyone for a prolonged time, not even a rich relative."

A small but genuine smile curved Garland's lips, and he nodded. "I've no intention of lingering any longer than I must. I cannot imagine this place is good for anyone's health, no matter their age. I am amazed Roderick has lasted as long as he has here. It must be musty and full of ill humors."

"Undoubtedly." I longed to kiss Garland's smiling lips, but there was no guarantee we were alone, despite the apparent emptiness of our surroundings. So I contented myself with a subtle caress of my hands down his arms, and then I stooped to retrieve my case. "Let's get on with it, then. Perhaps by this time tomorrow, we'll be shaking the dust of Bath from our shoes just like Reverend Whitefield."

Garland's amusement seemed to grow when he recognized the reference. "I am most eager to follow his example," he said as he approached the gate.

He nudged it open wider so we could pass through. I chuckled as I followed in his wake and stepped through the gate. Any levity I felt, however, died stillborn as I got my first good look at Heatherford House.

The wood of its facade was cracked and faded with only the faintest traces of whitewash. Despite its large and imposing structure, the grandeur it must have possessed a century ago had been diminished by time and the elements into naught but a memory. Here and there, the windows were cracked or broken, and I shuddered with a sense of foreboding as I gazed upward, fancying skeletal faces with empty eye sockets were staring back at me from behind every pane of glass.

But there was something beyond the miasma of age and neglect clinging to the house and grounds. The scent of death seemed to waft toward me as I stood staring at the house, and a chill rippled down my spine even as I told myself it was a fancy bred of failing light and

Garland's tales of drowned heirs. While a primitive part of my psyche wanted to take Garland by the hand and flee from this place as though the hounds of hell were nipping at our heels, I refused to be ruled by illusions and superstitions, like a Medieval peasant chanting prayers against demons lurking in the shadows.

"Obviously your uncle has saved part of his fortune by foregoing maintenance on the house," I muttered. "It would be wiser to knock it down and build anew than attempt to fix anything at this point."

"I may very well do just that if I inherit," Garland said as he continued along the overgrown walkway leading to the front porch. "The location itself has much potential, but the house..." He lifted his gaze from the porch to the roof and grimaced. "It is hideous."

"That it is." I lowered my voice, not wanting to be overheard by any inhabitants.

It seemed ludicrous that anyone could live in such a place, but we mounted the steps onto the porch and approached the front door. The wood was weathered but seemed sound, although it was the tarnished brass of the knocker which gave me pause. Garland must have felt the same, since he hesitated, seeming unwilling to touch the form of the misshapen, tentacled creature which served the prosaic function of a knocker.

"Is that...? What is that? It does not look like any sea creature I am familiar with." Garland touched the knocker with but two fingers to knock on the door.

"I have no idea," I replied, eying the knocker warily.

The brass landed with dull but loud thuds on the striker plate and then faded away into silence that stretched out for several moments.

I raised one eyebrow at Garland. "What shall we do if no one is at home?"

"Return to Bath and inquire about Roderick's solicitor, I suppose."

A flash of relief crossed Garland's face at the thought that we might have a reprieve from entering the derelict house. But his hope died when we heard shuffling footsteps approaching, and with a shriek of protesting hinges, the front door opened.

The first impression I received of Roderick's manservant was of long, lank blond hair and a beakish nose. His skin was pale, and he regarded us with one milky blue eye as he opened the door wider. The other eye was covered by a film of cataract. His clothes were creased and at least twenty years out of date. I fancied I could even see dust settled in the folds.

"May I help you?" The man's voice was high and nasal, grating to an ear more accustomed to harmonious sounds.

"My name is Garland Heatherford." Garland spoke with a strong, clear voice, showing no sign of unease now that we were in the presence of a stranger. "I was summoned as Roderick Heatherford's heir. This is my friend and colleague, Mr. Geoffrey Wainwright."

The manservant bared his stained and gapped teeth in what I supposed he considered a smile, and he shuffled out of the way. "Master Roderick is expecting you."

I would rather have walked into a blazing inferno than step through that dark, foreboding portal, but I had little choice save to square my shoulders and follow Garland into the house. I felt as though we were stepping into the maw of some slumbering beast, and the illusion was not lessened as my eyes adjusted to the dim interior, which was decorated in dusty, faded wallpaper of deep red. The floor was white marble that had been dulled and stained by time, dirt, and I knew not what else. Any hopes I'd had that the interior was in better shape than the exterior were dashed, and I glanced at Garland in dismay.

"Perhaps if your uncle will see you now, you can sign the papers, and we can return to town before dark?" I cut my eyes toward the manservant. "We don't wish to be a burden."

"The master has prepared for your arrival." The manservant beckoned to us to follow him deeper into the house. "My name is O'Brien. I will attend to you while you are here."

"I hope we do not require attending for long." Garland mustered a polite smile. "Are the papers ready?"

"That is for the master to say." O'Brien guided us toward the once-grand main staircase. "He is resting now. He will see you at dinner this evening."

I could not imagine what manner of food we would be served in these dubious surroundings, but I found myself reluctant to ask. Instead, we followed O'Brien up the creaking staircase to the second floor, which was carpeted with a stained and worn runner of an indeterminate color. We were led along the hall, and then O'Brien stopped before a door with a dusty glass knob.

"Young Master Heatherford, this is your room," he said as he pushed open the door. "The bath is the next door down. Mr. Wainwright will have the room beyond that."

I was loathe to be separated from Garland for even a brief time, but there seemed to be no help for it.

"I'll put my case in my room, then return so we can

talk," I said, offering Garland a reassuring smile. I had no wish for O'Brien to determine the exact nature of our relationship in case he carried tales to Roderick and thus disqualified Garland for his inheritance.

"Of course." Garland appeared no better pleased with the arrangement than I was, but he steeled himself and stepped into his assigned room, pointedly holding the door open when O'Brien offered to close it behind him.

O'Brien led me past the bath and opened the door just beyond it. I took a brief glance around as I stepped inside, but I did not wish to linger, even though the room appeared to be in better condition than the parts of the house we had seen so far. I dropped my case on the floor, and then I headed back into the hall, intent on returning to Garland's room.

"Thank you for showing us our rooms. I don't believe we require anything else." I raised my voice as I asked, "Do you need anything, Garland?"

"No, everything seems quite… adequate," Garland called back in a polite tone.

"Garland and I will be down when your Master is ready to see him, I think," I said, hoping O'Brien would take the hint.

I didn't care for the suspicious look on O'Brien's face, but I didn't have any desire to talk to the man any further. I was most relieved when he nodded and retreated back down the stairs. With a sigh of relief, I stepped into Garland's room, closed the door behind me, and locked it for good measure.

"My God."

"I hope He can still help us in this hellish place." Garland abandoned the pretense of opening his bag and hurried over to me, his arms outstretched. "Somehow I doubt it will be as quick and simple to extract ourselves from Heatherford House as we had hoped it would be."

I didn't hesitate to wrap my arms around Garland, and I held him tightly, needing the reassurance of that contact as much as he seemed to. "Despite your tales of death and darkness, I never thought the house would be like this."

"Razing it to the ground sounds like an excellent option right now." Garland leaned his head on my shoulder and released a long, slow sigh.

I searched for something positive to say, but it was difficult. "If your uncle will see you tonight, perhaps we can be gone on the morrow," I said, smoothing my palms up and down the length of his back. "But I tell you this: if you feel threatened in any way, we will leave. Even if it means leaving our things behind, we will go and damn the money and any future heirs. All right?"

"All right." Garland mustered a smile, a glimmer of relief in his eyes. "If we must stay overnight, could we share a room in secret? Perhaps I'm fretting for no good reason, but I would feel safer if we were not separated."

"That's an excellent idea." I smiled in return. "I'd rather be caught out and evicted from the premises for outraging your uncle than risk something happening to you that I could have prevented."

By silent consensus, we didn't bother to unpack our cases, since we hoped not to remain a moment longer than necessary. I took a cursory look at the bed linens, relieved to find them clean, if yellowed with age. The wood of the bed was in sad need of polishing, but the frame seemed sturdy enough to hold us both. With nothing else to do, we made our way back down to the first floor, seeking to satisfy our curiosity as to whether the entire house was as warped and ill-kept as what we'd so far seen. For the most part, the rooms seemed to have sat unused for years, judging by the depth of dust that had collected on every surface. The curtains were sun-faded and stained with mildew, as the climate this close to the coast was humid for much of the year. The furniture was made of dark, heavy wood, and all of it had split and cracked from lack of care. The cushions were frayed by time and possibly the depredations of rodents.

The one exception to the general aura of dilapidation was the library. This room alone seemed to have regular use. I smiled in delight when I saw the handsome, leather-bound tomes lining shelves which were all free of grime.

"Well, this is a happy surprise!"

"At least he has respect for something," Garland murmured, looking around the room with more genuine interest than he had shown for anything else. He went to inspect a nearby shelf, but the frown between his eyes deepened as he perused the titles. "Although these do nothing to set my mind at ease." He withdrew a black leather-bound book and held it up so I could read the title, which hinted at dark contents unfit for good men to read.

"Perhaps this helps to explain the drownings." I shoved my hands into my jacket pockets, unwilling to touch a single one of the books. "Your predecessors were so horrified and dismayed by the legacy they stood to receive that they attempted to escape via the river and met their doom."

Garland returned the book to its place and absently rubbed his hands on his waistcoat. "It would not surprise me in the least. This is far from the only book of its kind I can see on these shelves. Either Roderick is a collector of macabre, sinister works or…." He trailed off as if he was reluctant to voice his thought aloud.

I could not blame Garland for wishing to keep at least some illusion of normality in our most unusual situation. As it happened, it was just as well that he did not continue to speak, for the door to the library opened and O'Brien entered.

"The Master will see you now," he said, looking at Garland with a smile I found alarming in its smugness.

Garland squared his shoulders as he followed O'Brien out of the library, looking like a man being led to his doom. He glanced back at me as if to make certain I followed close behind. I had no intention of allowing him out of my sight, and I offered a smile of reassurance as I followed on his heels.

O'Brien led us to the dining room. While not in quite as much disrepair as the rest of the house, it was still dank and unpleasant, with dust and cobwebs festooning the wall sconces, highlighted by the gas lights.

My first impression of Roderick Heatherford was of immense age. Though well-groomed and dressed in an old-fashioned evening suit, the man in the wheelchair at the head of the dining table was so old, he seemed shrunken in around his bones, his pale skin hanging in lank wrinkles about his skeletal form, with wisps of white hair clinging to his bare pate. Indeed, he reminded me of the photographs I had seen of unwrapped mummies from Egypt, a comparison which made me shiver. Only his eyes, of a deep and fathomless black, seemed truly alive, and they focused on Garland with an avid interest.

"Good evening, Mr. Heatherford." Garland greeted his relative politely as if they had met at a fashionable party instead of this gloomy wreck of a room. "I am pleased to meet you at last."

"Good evening." Roderick's voice was creaky with age, but he made himself heard quite well. "We should not stand on ceremony, should we, since we are family? I remember your dear father as a boy. I shall call you Garland, and you must call me Roderick. Will you introduce me to your associate?"

Garland shifted uncomfortably, seeming unsettled by the familiarity. "Of course. This is Mr. Geoffrey Wainwright, my friend and colleague. I hope his presence is not an imposition, but we had planned to travel to Greece before we received your letter, and I asked him to accompany me here in recompense for cancelling the trip."

I could not say it was a pleasure to make Roderick Heatherford's acquaintance, so I pasted a smile on my lips and gave him a slight bow. "Good evening, sir."

"Good evening." Roderick turned to me, and I thought I saw a glitter of malice in his eyes before it disappeared, replaced by bland courtesy. "You are as welcome here as my dear nephew. Please sit, gentlemen." He gestured for Garland to take a seat at his right, and Garland complied without protest. "My cook has not had occasion to prepare a meal for guests since poor Orry died, and I suspect we are in for quite a treat."

I took the seat next to Garland, unable to imagine what kind of meal this Methuselah would consider a treat. But my thoughts were preoccupied by the ill will I'd sensed directed at me, and I kept a subtle eye on Roderick, alert lest my reluctant host decided to protest my presence and seek to remove me from the premises.

Much to my surprise, the first course proved to be a seafood bisque, smooth and creamy and seasoned with fresh herbs. I found it quite delicious, and while I remained on guard, my opinion of Roderick went up a grudging notch. The main course was sea bass, broiled expertly and served with potatoes and squash, and accompanied by an excellent white wine. For dessert there was sherry trifle, an elegant dish for such a small dinner.

Throughout the meal, Roderick kept up polite, almost charming conversation, expressing interest in Garland's academic career and talking of his own reading in Garland's field. Were it not for the initial glance he'd given me, I would almost have been willing to dismiss my first impressions of the house and its dilapidated state as being overblown.

Garland seemed to relax as the evening wore on, perhaps lulled into a state of complicity by our host's charm and helped along by the potent wine. His conversation grew animated, and he ate and drank with increasing appetite as his attack of nerves abated.

"I do apologize for the deplorable state of disrepair in which you find Heatherford House," Roderick said as O'Brien cleared away the dessert. "I was overcome by a lengthy illness. Indeed, my health is still fragile even now. My nerves sustained quite a shock at poor Orry's death, and I feel the reverberations still. Thus I have been unable to see to its care as I should have liked for quite some time."

"Quite understandable." Garland gave his uncle a

sympathetic smile. "Perhaps you could hire some workmen before winter sets in."

"Perhaps." Roderick's tone was absent, as if he had already dismissed the idea.

"In the meantime," Garland added delicately, "I wonder when we might meet with your solicitor? I appreciate your hospitality, Uncle, but I should not like to impose upon it too long."

"Mr. Banning was called away to attend to an elderly relative on her deathbed in Raleigh," Roderick said with slick glibness. "Rest assured, we will conclude the necessary paperwork at the earliest opportunity."

Garland's smile faltered, but he nodded acceptance of his uncle's words. "I am sorry to hear of his unfortunate errand."

"As am I, but death is part of life, is it not? We must accept our fate when it comes to meet us." Roderick's smile was bland, but his eyes glittered with a predatory light I neither understood nor liked.

Perhaps I should have held my tongue, but the comment seemed almost like a veiled threat, and I have no patience for people who cloak nastiness in honeyed words. Some imp of mischief took me, and I lifted my chin and surveyed Roderick boldly.

"I rather prefer John Donne's perspective on it," I said. "We can all look forward to that day when even death itself shall die."

"Indeed." Roderick's features darkened briefly before they smoothed out into blank courtesy again. "But you are young. Let us hope fate has long and happy lives planned for you both."

Garland dared to glance at me with his heart in his eyes as he raised his glass. "I will gladly drink to that."

I touched my glass to Garland's, using the excuse of leaning closer to put my hand on his leg and give it a brief, supportive squeeze. "A consummation devoutly to be wished." I sipped my wine, then glanced at Roderick. "If your solicitor is going to be away for some time, perhaps Garland and I should continue on to Beaufort, which we'd planned to do once your business was completed. We could spend a week there, and hopefully Mr. Banning will have returned by then."

Roderick leaned forward and clenched his fingers on the arm of his chair. "Perhaps," he said, a hard edge in his voice. "If Garland wishes to go there instead of remaining here and learning about the estate he will inherit."

I am not certain what surprised me more, the fact that Roderick was not pleased about my suggestion or that he would resort to such blatant manipulation. I bit my tongue to keep from uttering a sharp retort. This was not about me, after all, and I had no wish to put any stress on Garland by being at odds with his uncle. I was here to support and protect him, not make things more difficult.

"It was only a suggestion," I said, shrugging as though it didn't matter to me one way or the other. "I only thought to spare you from the rigors of entertaining guests for what might be an extended time, sir."

"Family is never an imposition." Roderick waved dismissively.

"Still, it might be more difficult than you anticipate, especially since you have been ill." Garland offered his uncle a placating smile. "Perhaps we will remove the burden from your shoulders and travel to Beaufort for a few days rather than an entire week, if that pleases you."

I said nothing but waited with interest to see what Roderick's response would be. I wondered if he was the sort of man who, once he had a person within his sphere of influence, had a pressing need to control them as much as possible. I'd seen the like before, particularly from my grandmother. The elderly so often enjoyed having the younger generations dance to their tune, and I wasn't surprised Roderick Heatherford seemed to be no different.

Instead of pressing the issue, however, Roderick reclined in his chair again and regarded Garland coolly. "If that pleases you, nephew, then I am pleased. No doubt Mr. Banning will have returned by then, and we can discuss the estate with him. I am certain he will be able to answer questions that I might not. I do not keep as close an eye on the books as I did in my younger days."

"That sounds perfect." Garland beamed, pleased at having reached a compromise, but I was not convinced Roderick had given in as easily as it appeared he had.

"Well, then, that's settled," I said.

I was pleased at the thought of escaping Heatherford House, even if we would have to return. Yet an inner voice urged me to caution, and I kept an eye on our host, waiting to see if he would do or say something to attempt to change Garland's mind about our plans. But nothing further was said about it, and not long afterward, Roderick excused himself, claiming an increased need for his rest. He bade us a good night, and then O'Brien wheeled him away. Roderick had his rooms on the first floor at the front of the house. At least Garland and I would not disturb him; our rooms were at the back overlooking the river, and we retired upstairs to Garland's room.

"Well. That was interesting," I said once we were alone behind a closed door.

Garland's lips quirked in a wry smile. "My uncle is not without his eccentricities."

I was pleased Garland was smiling, and I didn't wish to upset his calm by speaking of my own unease, so I kept my tone light. "We shall continue on to Beaufort in the morning, and I will admit I'm looking forward to it a great deal. It has been too long since I've seen the sea."

Garland moved closer and slid his arms around my waist, his smile widening as he gazed up at me. "It has been too long for me as well. Beaufort is a quaint town, and I look forward to visiting it again."

I wrapped my arms around his shoulders and rested my forehead against his. "It does not compare to Greece, but as long as I am with you, I am happy. What shall we do with the rest of our evening?"

"Select a book from my uncle's fine library?" Garland teased, giving me an arch look.

"I think not!" I laughed and hugged him. "Perhaps we should retire early, so we may rise and head into town as soon as it is light enough? I would like to ensure we get seats on the coach to Beaufort."

Garland nodded as he returned my embrace. "An excellent plan. I am eager to escape this dank, depressing house. I cannot bring myself to call it a home."

"I suppose you have no desire to live here once you inherit?" I didn't even try to keep the hope out of my voice.

"On the property, perhaps, and only if you are willing to move to the coast as well. It does have a lovely view of the water. However, if I inherit, the first thing I will do is raze this vile dwelling, burn the remains, and perhaps salt the earth for good measure."

"An excellent plan and one I will eagerly assist." I pressed my lips to Garland's, sealing the promise. "I suppose we should change for bed. I will muss the bed clothes in my room, then return, all right? I prefer not to let you out of my sight for a moment longer than I must."

Chuckling, Garland squeezed my waist and then released me. "I am more relieved than ever that I did not come here alone."

"As am I. I will return swiftly."

I hurried to my room and changed into my nightshirt, and then I drew back back the coverlet and shaped a dent into the pillow. Thankfully the bedrooms were in much better shape than the downstairs, but nevertheless I would sleep more soundly with Garland next to me. Within five minutes, I was back in Garland's room. I closed the door and locked it, giving us some degree of privacy.

Garland was already in his nightshirt and waiting for me in bed. He flipped back the covers, smiling a welcome at me. "Thank God we will not have to sleep apart while we are here. I do not think I would have been able to sleep at all without you beside me."

I slid into the bed and pulled Garland close. "I will keep you safe, love, and hold the nightmares at bay."

Garland nestled close and relaxed in my arms with the ease of familiarity. "I've no doubt my dreams will be far more pleasant with you here."

"As will mine." I reached out to extinguish the lamp, and then I relaxed against the pillows, drawing comfort from Garland's closeness. There was little I liked about either Roderick or Heatherford House, but Garland himself was a pearl beyond price. If there were nefarious forces at work, ones that may have harmed Garland's predecessors, I was going to do whatever I must to thwart them. No matter what.

CHAPTER 3

I would like to relate that Garland and I departed first thing in the morning and went to Beaufort, a seaside town of great charm, and we enjoyed a respite from Heatherford House. Unfortunately I cannot, for the ill luck plaguing everything having to do with Roderick Heatherford reached out to touch Garland.

Accustomed to rising early, I was awake just after dawn, and I kissed Garland softly. He muttered and turned away, and I chuckled, for Garland was not as enamored of mornings as I was. I rose and made my way back to the room I was supposed to have occupied in order to retrieve clothing, and then I repaired to the bathroom. After having shaved, washed, and dressed, I made certain O'Brien wasn't skulking about before returning to Garland's room.

I was surprised to find him still abed. Normally he was awake by the time I finished my morning preparations, and he would make his own while I attended to making coffee and breakfast for both of us. But my lover was lying just as I'd left him, and I hurried over, a shaft of fear stabbing through me at this departure from routine.

"Garland?"

I leaned over him and shook his shoulder. The morning sun was now shining through the curtains, and I gasped when I saw how pale his face was in the light. I checked to see whether he was indeed breathing. While his respirations were so low as to be hard to detect, he had not expired in the short time I'd been away from him. Nevertheless, I was quite alarmed and concerned, and I shook him harder.

"Garland! You must wake up!"

A faint frown creased his brow, and a moan escaped his lips, but he didn't open his eyes, and he made no other sound.

The icy fingers of dread touched me. I rested my hand on Garland's forehead, but he did not feel feverish to me; indeed, his skin was too cool to the touch, and I bit my lip, wondering what vile thing in this house had stricken him. That his condition was some part of our arrival at Heatherford House I had no doubt, and I hastened to open the door and peer into the hall.

"O'Brien! Hello! Can anyone hear me?"

O'Brien appeared a few moments later, slow to respond to my call, and he looked unconcerned despite the urgency in my voice. "May I help you, sir?"

"Mr. Heatherford is unwell," I said, frowning. "I need you to summon a physician at once."

"Of course, sir." O'Brien nodded, but he didn't exhibit any sign of alarm as he meandered back downstairs.

I tracked his movements, chafing at his slowness. "Do hurry!" I called after him, but I could do little else because some inner voice of caution warned me not to leave Garland alone and unprotected. I hated to depend on Roderick's manservant, but there was little help for it.

I returned to Garland and dragged a chair close to the bed. I clasped his hand between my own and chafed his wrist.

"Don't do this to me, love," I murmured. "Please, please, you must wake up."

The next hour was hellish. I continued to talk to Garland, worried he would slip away from me if I left him for even a moment. I glanced often at the door and at my pocket watch, wondering how long it would take for O'Brien to return with the doctor. The minutes dragged on until I was certain each one was going by more and more slowly.

Finally, however, my waiting was given a small reward. O'Brien still had not returned, but after lying as still as a corpse, Garland began to stir at last. It was slight at first—a crease of his forehead, a deeper indrawn breath, a restless movement of his hand—but I latched on to each tiny sign as though it were a lifeline drawing Garland back to me. I implored Garland to return, promising him anything and everything under the sun if he would only wake up and tell me he was all right.

Words cannot describe the depth of emotion which gripped me when Garland's eyes opened. Their crystalline blue was cloudy and dim, but I was so relieved at this sign of life that my voice grew hoarse, and my throat closed up. I still clutched one of his hands, and I reached out to caress his cheek.

"Please speak and tell me I'm not dreaming."

"Geoffrey?" His voice was weak, but he fixed his gaze

on my face with every sign of recognition. Whatever his ailment, he was not out of his head with a fever. "I feel unwell."

"You are unwell, although I know not what ails you." I brought Garland's hand to my lips and kissed it fervently. "I have never had such a fright in my life. You were cold and pale and still, and I feared I had lost you forever."

"I am weary, that is all," Garland said, giving my hand a weak squeeze. "I want to go back to sleep."

I knew what Garland had experienced was no natural slumber, but I didn't want to alarm him. I spoke with a soft and gentle voice. "I'm sure you do, love, but I've sent for a doctor to examine you. Does anything hurt? Do you feel ill at all?"

"I feel nauseated," he said. "Perhaps dinner did not sit well on my stomach. I thought the bisque tasted a little off."

The words made my breath catch. I had tasted nothing off about the soup, but I could not rid myself of the thought that either the cook or O'Brien had tampered with Garland's bowl but not mine. Garland, for all his delicate looks, had a hardy constitution and was rarely ill. I could not believe it was a mere coincidence he'd fallen ill within hours of our arrival. The only question in my mind was whether whoever had polluted Garland's food had done so on their own or had been acting on Roderick Heatherford's orders.

Unfortunately, there was little I could do. If I could have, I would have picked Garland up and carried him from the house, but without some means of transportation, I could not take him far. I could travel to town by myself and find a cart or a horse, but that would involve leaving Garland alone, and I was loathe to do so. There was no telling what might happen if I weren't around to keep Garland safe. I could only wait for the doctor and hope I could somehow alert him as to my suspicions without giving him the impression I should be locked up in an asylum.

"Perhaps so," I murmured, squeezing Garland's hand gently. "Are you thirsty? Would you like some water?"

He shook his head, and his eyelids began to flutter closed again. "No, just sleep."

I was dismayed Garland couldn't stay awake, but at least this time, his slumber seemed more natural. A bit of color had returned to his cheeks, and his breathing was deeper, and so I resigned myself to waiting for either the doctor to arrive or for Garland to wake once again.

It was almost noon before I heard footsteps coming up the stairs, and I sprang from my seat and hurried to throw open the door with eager haste. O'Brien stood in the hall, and with him was an older man, possibly in his fifties. He had iron gray hair, and he was dressed in sober black clothing with a leather bag clutched in one hand that indicated his profession.

"What seems to be the problem?" he asked, as I stepped back and allowed him into the room. "Mr...?"

"Wainwright," I said. "I am Mr. Heatherford's friend."

"I'm Dr. Hartman, personal physician to the senior Mr. Heatherford." He smiled benignly, but there was a shiftiness to his brown eyes that I didn't like.

"I came to awaken Garland so we could depart this morning," I said, "but I found him to be all but comatose. He wouldn't respond to my attempts to rouse him, and his skin was pale and cool to the touch. He was breathing so shallowly, I feared he might expire, so I called for O'Brien to summon a doctor." I allowed my gaze to move to the manservant, and I didn't bother to hide my animosity at his slow response to my request for assistance.

"Ah, quite wise." Dr. Hartman smiled again, but it didn't reach his eyes. "O'Brien had a hard time finding me. I was out on rounds, visiting some of my elderly patients. It was quite a lucky chance he found me at all."

I didn't believe the doctor's story, but Garland had need of his services, so I gestured toward the bed. "He woke up for a few minutes earlier and complained of nausea and sleepiness. He thought the soup we had at dinner last night didn't agree with him."

"Food poisoning, perhaps?" The doctor moved over to Garland and pressed a hand against his forehead. "No fever, but he appears warm and his breathing is fine." He glanced at me. "Are you certain he wasn't merely sleeping? Perhaps he was so deeply asleep, you couldn't rouse him. Some people are like that, you know. Their slumber is almost like being knocked out."

I started to say Garland didn't sleep that deeply, but I stopped myself, years of discretion stilling the words before I could speak them. I would have no reason, were I merely a friend and colleague, to know how deeply Garland slept. To indicate otherwise was to expose our relationship, and I was unwilling to do so lest Dr. Hartman refuse to assist Garland on the grounds of moral outrage. I had to content myself with shaking my head.

"No, I don't believe it was a natural slumber. I shook his shoulder repeatedly, and there was no response at all. When he did finally wake, all he wanted was to go back to sleep."

"Whatever it was, he seems all right now." Leaning closer, the doctor shook Garland's shoulder. "Mr. Heatherford? Sir, I need you to wake up."

It didn't take as long to rouse Garland this time, and when he opened his eyes, he appeared more alert. He frowned in puzzlement at the stranger bending over him, and he glanced at me for reassurance. "You are the physician, I presume?"

"Dr. James Hartman, your uncle's personal physician." Dr. Hartman patted Garland's shoulder. "It seems you have given your friend here quite a fright. How are you feeling?"

"Fatigued and a little nauseated," he said, struggling to sit up. "I believe I may have eaten some seafood that had gone bad last night."

"A sensible deduction, but I'll make sure nothing else is going on, shall I?" He helped Garland upright and shifted the pillows so Garland was propped up. He put his bag on the bedside table and began removing his implements.

"Are you all right with this, Garland?" I asked. I wanted to hold his hand and stroke his hair, but I couldn't. Instead, I kept half an eye on the doctor, still not convinced he wouldn't do something to make Garland worse instead of better.

"Yes, of course." I saw a flicker of doubt in Garland's eyes when he looked at Hartman. "If my illness is caused by something other than spoiled seafood, I would like to know about it."

"Certainly!" Hartman had donned a stethoscope, and he proceeded to listen to Garland's chest, but I saw his eyes shift toward O'Brien.

I stiffened, but I didn't turn around lest I betray I'd

seen the look. However, it was obvious to me Hartman knew quite well what had caused Garland's problems, but he wasn't about to tell us the truth.

Dr. Hartman went through the motions of an examination, and then he straightened. "Well, young man, I do believe you have the right of it. You had a bad reaction to the seafood, and your fatigue is caused by your body trying to recover from the toxins you ingested. Nothing to worry about at all, but you'll need to rest quietly for a few days. Plenty of bed rest, clear broth and tea when you are hungry. You'll be right as rain as long as you don't push yourself too hard."

Garland looked crestfallen, but he gave Hartman a resigned nod. "Thank you, Dr. Hartman. I am sorry you were called all the way out here for such a trivial complaint."

"It's no problem at all. I'm happy to give someone good news." Hartman packed his bag swiftly. "If you have any other problems, please send for me. I'm the only doctor in the area, so I'm quite busy, but I'll come as quickly as I can."

Then he was departed, and O'Brien followed him out. As soon as Garland and I were alone, I locked the door, and then I hurried back to the bed. I sat down and held out my arms to Garland.

"Oh, love, I was so worried about you!"

Garland moved readily into my embrace and leaned against me, releasing a long sigh. "But now we are trapped here. Perhaps I do not need as much rest as Dr. Hartman prescribed. If I feel stronger, we can travel to Beaufort tomorrow."

"As much as I hope we can, I will not risk your health."

I ran my hands over Garland's back soothingly. "You looked almost dead. I want to leave this place as much as you do, but we can't take a chance that whatever happened this morning will happen again, only worse."

"I suppose you are right." Garland sighed again, a resigned sound this time. "At any rate, I shall rest today and hope my health is better tomorrow."

"Indeed you shall, and I will attend to your food myself." I drew back and looked at Garland somberly. "I do not know for certain if your illness was due to misfortune or treachery, but I'm taking no further chances. I'd rather have your uncle think me rude and paranoid than risk anything else happening to you."

Garland raised a questioning eyebrow, but he didn't dismiss my statement or the implication behind it, which let me know he may have had similar thoughts. "I shall have my own taster, like royalty, or will you prepare my meals yourself? I would prefer not to risk both of us being incapacitated by *spoiled seafood*." His inflection on the words conveyed his doubt quite readily.

"I intend to make your meals myself, and I shall do so at times when you are awake and aware. In fact..." I paused for a moment. "I need to get my case, but I will be right back. All right?"

I rose and went to my room to retrieve my suitcase. I opened it and pulled out a smaller case, one I carried with me everywhere. I returned to Garland and sat down next to him again.

"I want you to keep this close, but don't let anyone see it," I said as I opened the case to reveal the small silver revolver within. "You know I'm not a man of violence, but there was a time when I felt my life was in danger because of my preferences, so I learned to shoot, and I bought this. I haven't felt the need for it since we've been together, but I believe in being prepared. After your talk of drowned heirs, I packed this."

Garland's eyes grew wide, and I thought perhaps he might protest such an extreme measure, but he held out his hands for the case. "My father taught me to shoot. I can use it, and I will if I must."

Apparently, there were still things for Garland and I to discover about one another. I passed him the case and leaned closer to press my lips to his forehead.

"I will feel better knowing you have this. When I prepare your meals or must otherwise leave your side, you will be able to protect yourself."

Garland closed his eyes and leaned into the kiss as he accepted the case. "I will keep it under my pillow while I am in bed and take it with me if I must leave the room alone."

"Excellent!" I smiled at him reassuringly. "Now we've settled that matter, what do you need? Shall I help you to the bathroom, or would you like some tea and broth?"

"The bathroom, please, and then rest," Garland said ruefully. "I am not yet hungry."

I helped Garland to his feet and kept one arm around him as we made our way to the bathroom. I didn't mind taking care of Garland, although I regretted the circumstance which necessitated it. I just hoped we would be able to escape from Heatherford House soon and return home so I could continue to care for Garland in surroundings where I would not also fear for his life.

CHAPTER 4

It was sometime after midnight when I woke, my slumber disturbed by a chill. I sat upright, heart pounding as I realized Garland's warm, familiar form was no longer pressed against me.

Moonlight streamed through the window, casting long, sharp shadows across the floor, and a chilly breeze, carrying the dampness of the river, swirled about the room. As my eyes adjusted to the stark glare, I noted with relief that Garland was standing in front of the window, staring out into the night. He was still and silent as a statue, and he resembled one as well, his skin and hair leeched of color by the moonlight until they were as pale as the cotton of his nightshirt. He was a beautiful statue, but the sight sent a chill through me colder than the night wind.

I threw back the coverlet and moved quietly up behind my lover. I wrapped my arms around his waist and drew him back against me. "Could you not sleep?" I asked, my lips close to his ear.

"The singing woke me up." His voice was soft and far away as if he was speaking from a dream, and he didn't turn his gaze away from the window. "Is it not beautiful?"

I strained my ears, trying to catch some trace of what he meant, but the only sounds I heard were the creaking and soughing of the wind in the trees and the low, faint susurrus of the river.

"I hear nothing but the wind and water," I said. "Were you dreaming, perhaps?"

"No, I can hear it now." Garland glanced back at me, frowning. "Can you not hear it? It sounds so beautiful and haunting. I have never heard its like before."

Again, I tried to catch some hint of what Garland seemed to hear so clearly, but I gleaned nothing from the night save the sounds of nature.

"No, I can't hear anything." I tightened my arms around him. "Perhaps your hearing is more acute than mine, and you've caught the voice of some boatman on the river."

Garland laughed and turned his attention back out the window, his gaze distant as if he saw as well as heard something I could not. "It is no man!"

I leaned my chin on his shoulder and nuzzled his ear. "Well, some boatman's wife, then. It is cold, love. I have no siren's song to lure you back to bed, but mayhap the promise of my hands on your body is enough of a lure?"

He had never hesitated to respond to my attentions before, but he did tonight, pausing for a long moment before tearing his gaze away from the window at last. "Yes, let us return to bed. The song is sweet, but your touch is sweeter."

And so we returned to bed, and I warmed Garland's

body with mine, coaxing sounds from his throat that were sweet to my ears. At last, he seemed sated and tired, and I curled myself around him as he relaxed against me. Yet even as Sleep wrapped her fingers around me, I noticed Garland's eyes were open, and he stared toward the window as though he were still listening to distant music.

CHAPTER 5

$\mathcal{M}$orning arrived with rain, imparting a damp chill to the room. I propped myself up on one arm so I could look down at Garland's face, relieved to see his beloved features were flushed with sleep rather than pale as they had been the previous dawn. I caressed Garland's cheek with one finger, enjoying the faint rasp of stubble and allowing myself a few luxurious moments to remember our closeness of the previous night. Finally, however, I leaned down and pressed a kiss to my lover's forehead.

"Garland, love, time to wake up."

Garland frowned and groaned, but this time, it was much more like his usual early morning protest than the sickly sound of the day before. When he cracked his eyes open, they were clear and focused, and his lower lip jutted a little.

"Must I? It seems I have only just gone to bed."

I could never resist Garland when he looked like a grumpy child, and I chuckled and gave his lower lip a playful nip. "And you shall remain in bed, but I need to get up, so you need to be awake enough to use what I gave you yesterday."

Garland yawned and rubbed his eyes, and then he sat up. "Could you help me to the bathroom first, please?"

I rose and moved to Garland's side of the bed so I could help him get up. I waited outside the bathroom while he completed his ablutions, and then I helped him back to bed. While Garland seemed more focused mentally, he was still weak, and I made certain he was comfortable and was able to reach the gun, although I hoped he wouldn't need it.

I rushed through my own preparations and checked on Garland again before making my way down to the kitchen, which was just below our bedrooms. A middle-aged woman was at the stove, poaching eggs, but she didn't turn around as I entered.

"Hello," I said, not wanting to startle her, but again she didn't seem to notice me. I moved closer, thinking perhaps the sound of the steadily pouring rain coming in through the open kitchen door was drowning out my voice. Yet it wasn't until I touched her on the arm that she glanced at me with a start.

"I'm Geoffrey Wainwright," I said. "Sorry to disturb you, but I want to make breakfast for the younger Mr. Heatherford."

She shook her head and touched her hands to her ears and then to her mouth. I was puzzled for a moment, and then it dawned on me: she was deaf and mute. She smiled at me with singular sweetness, and I smiled back. The problem was trying to communicate my needs to her. The previous day when I'd gotten broth and toast for Garland, the kitchen had been deserted, so I'd helped myself to what I needed. Garland and I both knew how to cook simple things, and I could prepare something that wouldn't upset his stomach. But I didn't want to get in her way and annoy her, risking the acquisition of yet another enemy in this house.

After making some motions to mime a stomachache and pointing to the bedroom above, she seemed to understand what I was asking for and motioned for me to take a seat at the table. While I would have preferred to make Garland's meal myself, I resigned myself to watching as she soft-boiled an egg and put some slices of bread into oven to toast.

Unable to sit still, I wandered around the kitchen. As I passed the door leading to the back porch, I looked outside, where the rain was still coming down. The boards of the porch were covered in the same weathered whitewash as the rest of the house, but that wasn't what caught my eye. The porch was dry, shielded from the rain by its roof, save for a damp swath which looked as though something had been dragged across it from the stairs to the door. There were streaks of mud as well, but the most disturbing thing was the sight of wet, muddy handprints on either side of the patch at regular intervals.

I frowned, trying to figure out who could have done it and how, and I stiffened as my mind called forth an image of Roderick Heatherford and his wheelchair. Could he have somehow dragged himself out of the house and then back inside, leaving this telltale trail to mark his passage? But why would he have done it?

If it had been Roderick, there should have been tracks in the kitchen as well. I looked at the floor, but there were no damp patches. Of course, the cook could have cleaned them up. I tapped the cook on the shoulder and pointed to the porch. She frowned, and I gestured at the floor, raising a brow.

"Did you see any tracks inside? Tracks like those?"

She shook her head, closed the door and locked it, and then she opened it again. I thought by this she was indicating the door was secured when she came into the kitchen that morning. She didn't seem disturbed by the tracks, and I wondered if odd occurrences were not out of the norm at Heatherford House.

The cook returned to the stove and her preparations. After pouring hot water in a porcelain teapot, she motioned toward a row of canisters whose neat labels indicated a selection of teas. I selected Garland's preferred type among them, and within five minutes, she handed me a bed tray with everything Garland needed. She added a bowl of porridge and a slice of ham for me, accepting my thanks with a smile.

I returned to Garland and closed the door behind me with a relieved sigh. "Everything in this house is an adventure, it seems."

Garland was sitting up in bed, one hand under the covers. As soon as I entered the room, he withdrew his hand and revealed he had been concealing the gun.

"What happened?" he asked as he returned the gun to its case.

I was both pleased and relieved Garland was taking his security so seriously. "I met the cook," I said as I brought the tray over to him and settled it across his lap. "I don't believe she had anything to do with whatever upset your stomach. Yet I did see something odd in the kitchen."

I described the condition of the back porch, as well as the cook's indication that whatever had made them hadn't come into the house.

Garland frowned, appearing as puzzled as I felt. "The only rational explanation I can think of is the tracks were caused by my uncle, but why would he be out there in the rain? It makes no sense. Little about this place does," he added with a sigh.

"Indeed. I cannot wait until we can return to our calm, rational lives." I gestured to the food. "You should eat and get your strength back to hasten that goal."

Garland eyed my ham covetously as he picked up a piece of toast. "I feel well enough to eat more than eggs and toast," he said, giving me a wide-eyed look of appeal.

I had no resistance against Garland when he looked at me that way, and I cut off a portion of the ham and rendered it into bite-sized pieces before putting it on the plate with his toast

"There. Just don't complain to me if you get a stomachache!" I groused playfully.

"I promise I will not." Garland favored me with a delighted smile and tucked into the ham, egg, and toast with every sign of satisfaction.

I ate my porridge, longing for the time when I'd be able to serve Garland breakfast in our own bed again. But my desires could not make the hours go by any faster, and so Garland and I remained in the room, occupying our time with reading and playing cards, and Garland napped on and off as fatigue took him.

The only disturbance we had was when O'Brien knocked on the door to inquire after Garland's health. I refused to let the man into the room and dismissed him by saying Garland was resting. I didn't like the smug smile on the manservant's face, but there was little I could do other than keep him as far away from Garland as I could.

As night drew in, the weather turned worse, with thunder and lightning combining with the rain and wind. Since there was no way of knowing if O'Brien had a key to the room, I wasn't certain if locking the door would be adequate to keep him out if he decided to seek entry. I am not certain why I felt O'Brien was a threat, but some instinct warned me O'Brien didn't have Garland's best interests at heart—or mine either, for that matter. Therefore, when we were ready to retire, I placed a chair before the door. It might not stop O'Brien if he was determined to gain entry, but it would at least slow him down and alert us there was mischief afoot.

Sleep was elusive for me, although Garland seemed to sink into slumber with relative ease. I lay for quite some time with my arm around his waist, staring at the window and watching the flares of lightning as they highlighted the waving branches of trees against the glass. I dozed from time to time, but I kept jerking awake, pulled back by sounds that set my nerves on edge.

I must have succumbed to fatigue at last, for I was startled to wakefulness by some instinct that had me sitting bolt upright in the bed, my heart pounding. I was immediately aware Garland was not in the bed with me, and it took me a moment of frantic scanning before I saw him standing before the door and trying to open it, thwarted by the chair. I sprang from the bed.

"Do you need the bathroom?" I asked, reaching out to touch Garland's shoulder.

But Garland showed no signs of responsiveness; he

did not even glance in my direction but continued to stare at the door and rattle the knob. I wondered if this was somnambulism, which I had read about but never before seen. Garland had never done such a thing before to my knowledge, and I was uncertain what could have triggered this event.

I wracked my brain, trying to recall what I had read, which had been little more than speculation and old wives' tales. I remembered there was something about not waking a sleepwalker, lest something unfortunate happen, yet were it not for the chair in front of the door, Garland might have already left the room and met some horrible fate.

What vision in his mind's eye had compelled him to leave the room? I wanted to know, but I was not going to move the chair and allow him to follow the fancies of his unconscious mind into mischief. I had to find some way to wake him gently or coax his thoughts in another direction.

"Garland, you shouldn't be wasting your strength on this. It's cold and you'll take a chill if you go about in bare feet. Come back to bed, and I'll warm you. You may sleep as late as you wish. I won't wake you early, I promise."

But my words fell upon deaf ears. Garland stared at the door for a moment longer, and then he began to hum a strange and haunting tune that chilled my soul. Grasping the knob with both hands, he began to shake and tug on it with all his strength, his determination to escape seeming to double.

Alarmed, I stepped forward, intending to take him by the shoulders, but I hesitated at the last moment, the half-remembered cautionary tales about sleepwalkers staying my hand. Yet if I could not force him away from the door, I'd have to coax him, and so I set out to do so.

"Where did you hear that song?" I asked, raising my voice in hopes of getting his attention. "I can't say I care for it much. It is far too melancholy. Do you remember the Chopin piece the pianist was playing when we met? I recall it well, and it has become one of my favorites because it reminds me of you, love."

I didn't know what to say, so I verbalized whatever came into my head, hoping that something—anything— would pull Garland's attention from the door. I told him how much I cared for him, how much I was looking forward to Greece, to returning home, to going anywhere that wasn't Heatherford House. Garland had always claimed to love my voice, and so I began to quote poetry to him: the sonnets of Shakespeare, the works of Byron, of Shelley, of the Greek masters. I do not know how long I stood there, talking to him, my mouth going dry with urgency to distract Garland from his attempts to leave the room.

At last, Garland let his hand fall away from the knob, and his humming faded into silence. He turned as if following the sound of my hoarse voice. There are no words to describe my relief when Garland gave up his attempt to leave. I reached out and gently, so very gently, took him by the hand.

"Let us go back to bed, love. You are still unwell. You need to sleep to get back your strength so we may leave this place."

He was quiescent now, allowing me to lead him back to bed and bundle him beneath the covers. I did not sleep, even when I had Garland held tightly in my arms so he would not try to rise again. It was not until Garland's body relaxed against me and his breathing came in the slow, steady rhythm of slumber that I allowed myself to draw in a breath and prepare to sleep once more.

Yet oblivion eluded me. My mind kept dwelling on Garland's uncharacteristic nocturnal perambulation as I tried to fathom a cause for it, and the tune he had been humming lodged itself in my brain, playing again and again without ceasing. The notes followed no pattern or scale in my experience, but conveyed a sense of both melancholy and menace, and I found myself disturbed by them, and even more by the mystery of where Garland could have heard them in the first place.

These unproductive ruminations kept me from slumber, yet I must have dozed, for I woke with a start, surprised to see the sky had lightened outside, although the storm continued unabated. Garland still slept, so I disentangled myself, allowing him to rest after the upset of the night. A glance at my pocket watch indicated it was long past the time I was accustomed to rising, yet I did not feel refreshed. Tension and worry sat upon me like a dark cloud, and I dared not allow myself to hope that we might make our escape from Heatherford House this day.

I removed the chair from before the door, chilled to see the lock was no longer engaged. Whether Garland had managed to somehow rattle it free or a key from without had been employed, I could not determine. Frowning, I sat in the chair, prepared to wait until Garland woke before seeing to my own needs.

It wasn't long before he awoke and favored me with a sleepy smile. "Good morning, love."

I moved to sit on the bed and brushed a lock of golden

hair back from Garland's forehead. "Good morning. How did you sleep?"

He reached for my hand and brought the back of it to his lips. "Well enough, although I feel tired still." He peered up at me, worry lurking in the depths of his eyes. "You do not look at all well rested. Did I disturb your sleep?"

I debated what I should tell him. Finding out one has walked about at night without one's knowledge seemed as though it would be rather disturbing, and with Garland still recovering from his illness, I thought it best not to upset him. So I smiled and shook my head, promising myself I would tell him everything once we were safely home. "No, it was the storm. Can you believe it is still shows no sign of abating?"

He glanced out the window, then looked back at me with dismay. "We will not be able to leave today, will we?"

I squeezed his hand. "I fear not. I doubt your uncle would give us use of a carriage even if he had one, and you are in no shape to walk through the rain. But we are safe enough for now as long as we keep our guard up. The storm must slacken eventually, and you are becoming stronger bit by bit. By tomorrow or perhaps the day after at the latest, we shall depart. Then if your uncle still desires to make you his heir, he can send the papers to you, and you can sign and return them. If he does not, well, who would be next to inherit? If you warn them, at least they will be on their guard."

"I do feel better than I did yesterday," he said. "If the solicitor has not returned by the time I am well enough to travel, I will insist on the papers being sent to me rather than remain a moment longer. If that disqualifies me as an heir, so be it. I will seek out my second cousins and warn them to be wary if they are approached." He peered out the window again and shuddered, and when he looked back at me, his eyes were haunted. "I wish we could leave. I grow weary of this wretched place."

"As do I." With another squeeze, I released his hand and rose. "As you are feeling better and are awake, I shall go and fetch your breakfast. I believe the gun case is still beneath the pillows. Will you be all right until I return?"

"Yes, I will be fine." He offered a reassuring smile that faded at the edges as he watched me move away from the bed. "Do hurry back."

I summoned up a smile of my own. "Of course. As swiftly as I possibly can."

It took me only a few minutes to change clothing, and then I made my way down to the kitchen. Given it was nearly ten o'clock, I was not surprised to find the kitchen empty and the stove cold. Undaunted, I set about making eggs and slicing bread and ham.

So focused was I on completing my task, I didn't notice the smell at first. It crept up on me gradually, a sour, fishy undertone to the scents of the food I was preparing. Although I am not certain why my brain made a connection, I thought of the odd tracks on the porch the previous morning, and so I opened the kitchen door.

The scent came more strongly then, and I stepped out onto the porch, wondering if the river had overflowed and we were in danger of being flooded. But the rear lawn and garden, although rain-sodden, seemed quite normal. Or it did, until I noticed the silvery, oblong forms on the lawn were not rocks as I'd first thought. They were fish—

hundreds of them of every shape and size, but all of them still and dead.

I gaped at the horrific sight. What bizarre twist of nature could possibly have stranded that many fish so far above the river? There was no other debris that I could see, no other flotsam that would have indicated the area had flooded and then receded during the night. There was nothing but the fish, their unseeing eyes turned up to the sky and mouths agape where they'd suffocated in the humid air.

I could not wrap my mind around the occurrence, so I stepped back inside the house and closed the door. I was no student of the natural sciences, and I could not think of any possible way the fish could have been deposited upon the lawns without any evidence of the method of their arrival.

I returned to the room and settled the bed tray with Garland. Once the door was locked, I moved to the window, wondering if the higher perspective of our room would give some further hint about the fish and their strange deaths.

"What is it?" Garland asked, seeming more interested in what I was doing than in his food. "Is someone out there? Has the solicitor come?"

"I fear not." I bit my lip as I tried to formulate some description that made logical sense. But there was none. "This place continues to prove a horror. There are dead fish outside. I know not how many, but the back lawn is covered to them all the way down to the water."

Garland put aside the tray and flung back the covers, and he climbed out of bed with the clear intention of seeing this new marvel for himself. "Were they blown up by the storm, do you think?"

"I cannot see how." I stepped back from the window to make room for Garland beside me. From this perspective, I could see the fish all the way to the trees at what I assumed was the edge of the property. "Why only fish? No weeds, no mud, no branches. Nothing but fish."

Garland stood close and slid his arm around my waist, his eyes growing wide as he gazed down at the macabre sight below. "A mystery indeed and a horrific one," he murmured. "Would that we had never heard of Heatherford House!"

"Indeed." I turned away from the death below and pressed my lips to Garland's forehead. "You should eat now. The sooner you are well, the sooner we can leave."

He dragged his gaze away from the window. "Excellent incentive indeed," he replied as he returned to the bed and retrieved the tray. His appetite seemed much improved, and he ate heartily until his plate was empty.

I had made toast for myself, but my appetite was less keen, although I forced myself to eat one slice. When Garland was finished, I unlocked the door long enough to place the tray out in the hall before closing the door and locking us within again.

"What would you like to do today?" I asked.

"Perhaps I could sit up for a while, and we could play cards." Garland gestured to a table on the other side of the room that was large enough for two to play at cards comfortably. "I do not think that will tax my strength overly much, and I will tell you when I grow tired."

We spent the rest of the morning and into the early afternoon thus engaged. I retrieved lunch for us, but there was still no sign of the cook I'd met the day before. One person I did see, however, was O'Brien. He was out in the rain with a wheelbarrow, collecting the fish and carrying them off I know not where. He'd made progress, but I did not envy him the task, especially as the thunder and lightning had continued unabated.

But with O'Brien thus occupied, I relaxed enough to nap with Garland for a short time after lunch, although I did put the chair in place at the door. When we woke, I spent the afternoon reading to Garland, who begged me to do so. I couldn't deny him, although I had to steal frequent sips of water to ease my throat, which was still a little rough from all the talking I'd done during the night.

"I hope you are not taking cold." Garland watched me with concern as I took another sip of water. "Perhaps some hot tea with honey would help."

"I will be fine." I smiled at him reassuringly. "I will prepare some tea when I go down to fetch our supper, I promise."

It was nearly dark when I called a halt to the reading, standing up and stretching before I moved to look out of the window. O'Brien had cleared most of the fish that I could see, and I suspected he was far more in danger of taking cold than I was, after hours in the pouring rain. I might even have felt a twinge of sympathy for him, despite my visceral dislike of the man.

"I'll be right back with our dinner." I bent to kiss Garland on the forehead and left him, again locking the door behind me.

I made my way downstairs, and as I stepped into the foyer, I saw O'Brien walking through the sitting room. He hadn't noticed me, and so I followed him, keeping myself as out of sight as I possibly could. I did not wish an encounter with the man, but I was curious about what he was doing.

Past the sitting room was a hallway with what appeared to be a single door at its end. As I drew closer, I thought I heard strains of music, and I stopped as O'Brien reached the door. I peered around the edge of the sitting room wall and watched as he opened it. The music grew louder, a piano piece I did not recognize, played at high volume and with a great deal of pathos. Then the door was shut, and the music muted. It had to be a gramophone, for I doubted a man of Roderick's age and infirmity was capable of playing any instrument with such vigor. But there was no way to satisfy my curiosity, so I headed toward the kitchen.

There was still no sign of the cook, and I wondered what Roderick had been doing for meals. My curiosity, however, was not so great that I felt inclined to seek out the man and inquire, despite his invalid state. O'Brien seemed capable of caring for his master, and they probably desired my help as little as I wished to offer it.

After a swift examination of the larder and the ice box, which was growing empty, I found some cooked beef that seemed decent enough, and after tasting it and deciding it was not tainted, I settled on sandwiches for our supper. One thing was becoming clear to me, however: even if Garland was not fully recovered on the morrow, we must leave before food became scarce. Either deliveries were suspended due to the storm or the absent cook brought supplies with her, but if the storm did not blow itself out soon, we might end up going hungry.

After our meal, I helped Garland to bathe. He was

much stronger, it was true, but I did not wish for a sudden bout of unexpected vertigo or nausea to result in a tragic accident. When he was clean and changed into his night-shirt, I helped him back to bed.

I was tired after my sleepless night, so we retired early, but despite my fatigue, I once again found sleep elusive. I found myself tensing, waiting for the next bizarre occurrence to make itself known, and, unfortunately, my expectations were not far off the mark.

Full darkness had fallen, and I watched the lightning. It seemed as though the storm was growing stronger, and I could hear the old house creaking and groaning from the force of the wind, and beyond that, I heard the snap and crack of tree branches. This, then, was probably a hurricane, one of the monstrous storms that blew in from the ocean, sinking ships and sometimes even wiping entire towns off the face of the earth. I silently prayed we would not meet with such a fate.

As I lay there, I felt Garland beginning to stir, and I tightened my arms around him. Garland struggled to sit up, and I suspected he was having a recurrence of what-ever nightmare had possessed him the previous two nights. Indeed, he began humming now, the same strange, haunting tune from the night before.

"Shh… hush now." I could not say why I found a simple tune so dangerous, but I recalled tales of music luring men to their deaths in far too many legends and fairytales to be comfortable with Garland's repetition of the song, if song it was and not the product of a brain being driven close to madness.

But Garland continued to resist my attempts to restrain him, his struggles growing ever more frenetic.

He whimpered and moaned between humming snatches of the tune as he reached out toward the window, and his efforts to free himself became tinged with desperation.

I was desperate as well, for I feared he might do himself great mischief in his present state, perhaps even hurl himself through the window in his frantic efforts to escape. I could not allow it; to keep him safe was the reason I had come with him in the first place, only I had not expected to save him from himself.

I pinned Garland's arms against his sides and pressed him down onto the mattress with my body, as I cast about desperately for a way to distract him or restrain him without causing him injury. I attempted to talk to him as I had the night before, but the lure of the voices must have been too strong, for he did not cease in his struggles to free himself.

A glance around the room showed me nothing I considered of any use, but when my gaze fell on the pillows, it occurred to me that perhaps I could use the cases to fashion restraints. I hated to tie Garland down, but if it was that or lose him, I knew there was but one choice I could make. Being larger and heavier than Garland, I was able to pin him with my weight, and I released his hands so I could strip away one of the pillowslips. After a struggle, I regained my grasp of Garland's wrist, and I wrapped it with the sturdy cotton and tied it to the iron bedframe above his head.

Garland yanked at his new bonds and thrashed beneath me, desperate cries rising from his throat. I begged his forgiveness, explaining I was only doing it to keep him safe. I coaxed and cajoled and pleaded for his understanding, even as I removed another pillowslip and bound his other wrist as I had the first.

Once he was restrained, I moved off Garland, still imploring him to listen to me and not to the crooning voices. I left the bed long enough to retrieve my belt, which I then used as a strap to bind his ankles to the rail at the foot of the bed. Garland's struggles grew weaker, although he writhed helplessly for a minute or two longer before falling silent and still at last. He rolled his head on the pillow and stared at the window, and he began to hum again, a mournful sound of pure longing.

My heart ached, but there was nothing I could do other than to crawl back into the bed with him. I lay close and stroked Garland's hair, imploring him to listen to me. The door rattled on its hinges, and I sat up in alarm and watched the doorknob turning in one direction and then the other. My heart pounded, for I could not imagine any beneficent purpose behind someone trying to get into Garland's room at this hour. I was glad indeed the door was both locked and barricaded with the chair, although I reached for the gun in case the intruder was determined enough to get past the obstacles. But after a short time, the doorknob went still and did not turn again, and I turned my attention to Garland once more.

Sometime after midnight, the storm grew even more violent, and the wind gusting around the eaves sounded like the voice of a woman wailing. Garland relaxed, and with a sigh, he sank into what seemed to be a deep slumber.

I was much relieved by this, even though the violence of the storm increased to the point that the protestations of the old house sounded like the moans and shrieks of a soul in pain. But those noises were natural, and they did not chill my soul as had Garland's eerie tune.

Lying beside Garland, I wrapped my arm around him and nestled close. I dared not untie him, not while it was dark outside. He seemed well enough in the daytime with the obsession only troubling him at night, so bound he would remain until the sun had risen.

The night seemed endless, as I counted each of Garland's slow respirations, unable to close my eyes for fear Garland would work himself free and be gone before I woke. But one thought was fixed in my mind, and I would not be swayed: we would leave on the morrow, even if I had to carry Garland through the storm. It was safer for Garland to face the whims of nature than continue to suffer whatever shadow this place had laid upon his mind.

I checked my pocket watch often, knowing sunrise occurred around six o'clock in the morning. When it was a quarter past the hour, I untied Garland slowly and carefully so as not to rouse him. I thought it best to do so before he woke and wondered what had happened. It seemed to me best to explain when we were well away from this place and the danger it presented to the man I loved.

He slept a while longer, and when he began to stir at last, he woke slowly. His face was bleary, and his eyes were cast in shadow as if his nocturnal struggles had weakened him anew.

"What time is it?" he asked, lifting one hand to his head as if it ached. "I feel as though I have barely slept all night."

"It is nearly seven," I said, reaching out to touch his forehead gently, hoping I had not been the one to cause his pain. "It was not a restful night, I fear. Did you not hear the storm? I suppose this house is far sturdier than it appears to have survived this weather without blowing down around our ears."

"Perhaps the storm is what disturbed my sleep," he murmured as he sat up and pushed back the covers. "I feel better, merely ill rested."

I was relieved by this assertion. "Do you feel well enough to leave today? I have had my fill of this place."

Garland hesitated before replying, showing a reluctance I didn't expect. "Perhaps, but we have been here this long. It seems fruitless to leave now when the solicitor may arrive at any time, and there is the weather to consider as well."

I stared at him in dismay, unable to believe after everything that had happened, Garland wasn't already out of bed and getting dressed so we could depart. But Garland knew nothing of his nocturnal wandering. It appeared I must divulge the trials of the previous two nights to encourage his cooperation, but I was loathe to do so, lest I distress him too much. We were both tired, and my thought processes had become slow, my logical mind overcome by the urge to escape this place as soon as possible.

Pinching the bridge of my nose, I tried to assemble my thoughts into some form of coherency and not give in to the desire to scoop Garland up and rush out into the storm. Garland was right in that regard, and I cared less about the possible arrival of the solicitor than I did about one or both of us being killed by a falling tree.

Finally, I nodded. "You are right, of course. If you are feeling well enough, perhaps we could go downstairs? I will prepare us something to eat, and we can find out if there is any hope of this storm ending soon."

Garland climbed out of bed, seeming eager to put my plan into action. "An excellent notion. I feel quite well enough to dress today, and I would like to enjoy a view of something other than these bedroom walls."

This display of energy was a definite improvement over the pale and tired countenance Garland had sported for two days. I dressed as well, although a glance in the mirror over the dressing table showed I was rather more worse for wear than Garland appeared to be.

Once we were ready, we descended to the first floor, and I was immediately assaulted by the odor of wet decay. My stomach rolled, and I took a handkerchief from my and covered my nose.

"Could that be the fish from yesterday?" I wondered aloud. "My God, what a stench!"

Garland recoiled with his hand over his nose as he searched for his own handkerchief. "It smells like more than rotting fish. There is something else—something earthy, wet, and foul."

"Is there no end to the horrors of this place?"

I headed toward the kitchen. Unsurprisingly, there was no cook, but I had reached the conclusion she did not live in the house and must come in each day. Yet the back door stood open, and there were muddy footprints on the floor. I stepped around these, not wishing to pick up the evil substance on my shoes, and craned to look out the door.

What had been fish-covered lawns the previous morning were now a mud and slime covered expanse. There were fish caught in the mess, to be sure, as well as river vegetation, tree branches, and unidentifiable lumps I didn't care to contemplate too closely.

"The river must have flooded during the night," I said.

"I wonder if this happens with every severe storm." Garland peered outside, grimacing with disgust, and then his eyes widened in alarm, and he pointed at a patch of ground near the steps. "Good God! Are those human bones?"

The light outside was dim and grey, but a sudden flash of lightning suddenly threw into relief the sight which had caught Garland's eye. At first glance, it appeared to be a smooth white stone, buried in the muck but washed clean by the rain. But as I stared at it, the form became more obvious: a skull, its sightless eyes turned toward us. Yet there was more than merely a skull; there was a whole skeletal form. Tattered rags held the bones together, and although it must have been tossed up from the river by floodwaters, the appearance suggested it was crawling toward the steps of the porch, one arm outstretched as though it had been halted in its progress.

I am not a religious man, considering myself a rationalist who did not need the trappings of superstitious beliefs to provide comfort. Despite this, I crossed myself, something I had not done in years, my hands trembling as I went through the motions.

"It must have been someone drowned and lost years ago," I murmured, unable to tear my eyes away from the sightless sockets that seemed to be staring right at me.

Garland appeared as transfixed by the gruesome sight as I was. "I hope my uncle will see to it they are given a proper burial at last."

"That would be the right thing to do." I stared outside

into the rain for a few moments, and then I stepped back and closed the door. "It must have been a flood." My thoughts still felt slow. I was missing something, but I couldn't think what it might be, and my head was beginning to throb. "We should eat, if you can manage it with this stench in the air."

"We can try." Garland withdrew into the kitchen, averting his gaze from the briny muck. "Perhaps our noses will adjust quickly."

"We can only hope." I found a towel and wiped up the muddy prints, and then I tossed the filthy cloth out on the porch. Between cutting off the air from the back and removing the filth, the air seemed less foul, at least by comparison. Then I dove into the pantry once again and was fortunate enough to find tins of flour and sugar. "What do you say to flapjacks?"

"I say yes." Garland tucked his handkerchief back in his pocket and approached the stove. "May I be of any assistance? You have done so much for me these last few days, and I should like to make myself useful."

"You may get the eggs and milk from the icebox and pray they have not turned bad," I said.

I found the act of cooking soothing, the prosaic normality of the actions providing a distraction from the fact that there was a dead body not twenty feet from the back door. But there was nothing I could do for that poor, long dead soul, and taking care of Garland was an activity far nearer and dearer to my heart. Some might think me cold for continuing with such a mundane task, but between fatigue and the surrealism of all that was happening to us, I clung to the things I was comfortable with and understood.

But if cooking in the vicinity of a corpse was acceptable, eating was not. We had grown accustomed to the smell by this time, but once our meal was prepared, I motioned toward the dining room. "Let's eat elsewhere, shall we?"

Garland acquiesced readily to my proposal, and he helped carry our repast into the dining room. His appetite was healthy, and color was returning to his cheeks. He seemed in higher spirits as well, although whether it was due to the meal or the change of scenery, I could not say.

The light of the gas lamps was highlighted by the steady flicker of lightning. We did not hurry over the meal, since there was little point in rushing when we had little else to occupy our time. While normally a man who preferred the peace and quiet of a library to the hustle and bustle of city streets, I'd had enough seclusion to last for quite some time. What I would not have given to walk away!

After our meal, we took what bit of exercise we could by walking around the first floor of the house, stopping to wonder at the curious pieces that caught our attention. I even showed Garland the door I thought led to his uncle's rooms, and we listened intently, catching the faint strains of a piano concerto.

"He must have a gramophone," I said. "Surely a man of his age isn't playing a piano himself!"

"I cannot imagine he is." Garland cocked his head quizzically. "He must have it quite loud for us to hear it out here. I wonder if he is going deaf."

"Perhaps so." I put my hand to my forehead. Again, I had the sense there was something I was missing, something fatigue had blurred from my inner vision. Yet surely there was a rational explanation for the recent events, even as bizarre as it all seemed. "Perhaps he doesn't care for the sound of the storm. Many people are frightened of thunder and lightning."

"That is a likely possibility as well." Garland turned away from his uncle's door. "Given what it has left in its wake, I cannot say I am fond of the storm either."

We continued to our exploration and ended up in the dank foyer where we'd first entered. The place looked no more welcoming than it had the first night. Yet as we stood there, peering into the dim corners, a clatter came from outside that had us running to the windows, where my eyes were greeted by one of the most welcome sights I could ever remember seeing: a carriage, drawn by soaked and stamping horses, which stopped before the porch. The chariot of Apollo could not have been more welcome to my sight.

"Can it really be?" I muttered. "Please tell me I am not dreaming!"

Garland's face was alight with hope as he crowded at the window next to me. "There is a man alighting. He does not look much like the doctor. Does he?" he asked, seeming uncertain. "My memory of that day is somewhat blurry."

"No, that is not the doctor."

Of this I was certain, although I could not see the man's face, obscured as it was by the umbrella he was holding. But this man was taller and broader than Hartman. He made his way through the deluge to the porch, almost losing the umbrella in a sudden wind gust. I did not care who it was, since his arrival would likely be the chance for our own departure. I hurried to the door and fumbled with the lock before wrenching the heavy thing open at last.

The stranger was closing his umbrella, and he glanced at me, raising one eyebrow. "Well, well, either O'Brien has gotten better looking, or you must be Garland."

"Neither actually." I stepped back and beckoned to Garland. "I am Garland's associate, Geoffrey Wainwright. And you are…?"

"Frederick Banning, Mr. Heatherford's solicitor." He stepped into the foyer, a large, bear-like man with dark hair greying at the temples. "Beastly weather! It was sunny when I left Raleigh!"

"I am Garland Heatherford." Garland stepped forward eagerly, his hand outstretched. "It is a pleasure to meet you, Mr. Banning. Thank you for coming all this way in such a storm."

Banning sized Garland up and then offered his hand. "Roddy was most anxious to have these papers signed by today if at all possible. He's an old client of mine, so I do my best to humor him. He likes everything to be in order, given the size of the estate. He fears it being chopped up among the various members of the family if he doesn't have a properly designated heir who understands how important it is to keep everything together."

Personally, I thought the large fees Mr. Banning likely received for handling the matters of the estate had as much to do with his eagerness to see to Roderick Heatherford's wishes as anything else, but I held my tongue.

"Of course." Garland nodded politely, although from the knowing look he gave me, I could guess he was thinking about our conversation concerning the house and the razing thereof. "I am most eager to have the paperwork in order myself. This has been an *interesting* idyll, but I must return home to begin preparing for the next term."

"I can imagine." Banning seemed sincere, there was something about him I didn't trust. Perhaps it was my fatigue speaking, or it could have been his assertion that Roderick was a longtime client, and I didn't trust Roderick. But now he was here, the papers could be signed, and Garland and I would be free.

Banning moved to the door and waved to his coachman. "Matthew will go to the coach house. No sense making the horses stand in the weather, after all. The paperwork will require many signatures and you'll want to read it over, of course."

"Indeed I will. I mean no offense to you or to my uncle, but you will understand if I have no desire to sign anything I have not read or do not fully understand," Garland said.

"Excellent!" Banning clapped Garland on the shoulder in a familiar manner, and then he sat his case on the floor and shrugged out of his wet coat and draped it over the bannister. "O'Brien must be in with Roddy. Let me go see if he feels up to a meeting." He sniffed and wrinkled his nose. "Ah, the river must have flooded again. One of the dangers of living close!"

He moved off, seeming familiar with the location of Roderick's rooms, and I turned my attention to Garland.

"At last! It seems we will be shaking mud rather than dust off our shoes, but I'm glad we may depart soon."

"As am I." Garland's answering smile was suffused

with relief. "I will be most pleased to settle the matter at last."

"Definitely." I placed both hands on Garland's shoulders. "Then we can return home and make plans for Greece once again. I suppose it will have to wait until next summer, but it will happen."

"Indeed it will. I think we deserve a proper holiday after this." Garland covered my hands with his, his eyes warm with affection as he gazed up at me.

I longed to kiss Garland's smiling lips, but that would have to wait, for I heard the sound of a door closing. I stepped back as Banning returned to the foyer.

"Thankfully, Roddy feels well enough to confer with us," he said, rubbing his hands together as though he was eager to get started. "If you'll come with me, Garland, we'll have this finished in a matter of hours."

"Of course." Garland moved away from me with reluctance.

I made to follow them, but Banning frowned at me and held up one hand as if to ward me off. "This will take some time, Mr. Wainwright. Family matters, you know. I'm sure you understand the need for discretion."

I halted in my tracks, an objection rising to my lips but dying unspoken. What could I say? Society would never recognize the claim Garland and I had on each other, nor my right to be by his side to support him. But more than that, I did not wish to let Garland out of my sight, to have him in the rooms of his uncle where I would not be able to help him if he needed it.

I looked at Garland, and I know my expression was desperate. It was up to him now, it seemed; if he had an objection or felt in danger, surely he would protest my exclusion.

Garland hesitated, but then he gave me an apologetic look. I could well imagine he was wary of revealing how close we were to a stranger; after years of careful discretion, the instinct to hide and be cautious was ingrained in us both.

"I will be fine," he said.

If I protested, it would do no good and possibly end up prejudicing Banning against Garland. I couldn't do that, and so I pasted a smile on my lips. "Of course. I'll pack my things, then. Assuming you wouldn't mind giving us a lift into town when your business is finished, Mr. Banning?"

"You're going to leave today?" Banning seemed incredulous. "But there won't be a coach for a couple of days, I'm sure, given the storm."

"Yes, well, we've already remained longer than we had planned," I hurried to say. "Perhaps you're wrong about the coach, and I would hate to miss it."

Banning didn't seem pleased, but then he shrugged. "Very well. It won't be easy going into town, but there is room in my carriage, if you're so determined." He glanced at Garland. "We'd best get started if we wish to be finished before dark."

"I'm ready, Mr. Banning," Garland said firmly, gesturing for Banning to precede him to Roderick's door. "I'll be as quick as possible," he added, glancing back at me.

Watching Garland walk away without voicing an objection was difficult to do, but years of discretion stilled my tongue, and I winced at the sound of the door closing behind him.

At a loss, I stood in the middle of the foyer, listening to the wind and rain and thunder. It seemed the storm might be slackening off, a circumstance that gave me a feeling of relief. I should be dancing a jig at the thought of leaving, but I was far too worried about Garland to celebrate prematurely.

"What can happen to him with the solicitor right there?" I murmured, trying to put my trepidation aside. I pinched the bridge of my nose and tried to convince myself I was suffering from a lack of sleep and an excess of paranoia, the remedy for which was sleep. But there was no way under Heaven I could sleep now, lest something happen that would find me unable to react. So action it would be, and I mounted the stairs and went back to our room, deciding to pack up our things in order to hasten our departure once Mr. Banning was satisfied with his paperwork.

It didn't take long to deal with our luggage. I retrieved the gun case and stared at it for a long moment, biting my lip in indecision. Paranoia might be affecting my decisions, but it seemed to me an excess of caution was hardly a liability, so I slipped the gun itself into a pocket of my jacket, then packed the case away and carried our belongings down to the foyer.

I prowled around the first floor and walked several times past the door to Roderick's rooms, hearing the sounds of piano music but nothing else. The door must be quite thick to block even the murmur of voices, and I sighed unhappily before resuming my restless wandering.

It was on my third turn through the library that a sudden flare of lightning threw the room into relief and brought something to my attention I'd not noticed before.

On the far wall of the room, which seemed, by the house layout, to have abutted the kitchen pantry, there was a gap between the western wall, whose windows overlooked the river side of the house, and the first set of bookcases along the northern wall. The bookcases were wide and quite deep, and so it was not at first apparent that an opening of some two feet or so existed, until the lightning made it stand out. I moved toward it, wondering what the odd niche contained, and I was quite surprised to see a narrow door, recessed at the depth of the bookcases, not hidden but not apparent unless one was either at the western wall or looking at the last bookcase directly.

For a short time, I contemplated the door, wondering at its odd position. Perhaps it predated the use of this room as a library, although what its purpose could be I couldn't have said. I stepped closer, fitted myself into the narrow space, and grasped the doorknob.

At first, I thought the door was locked, since the knob didn't yield to my attempts to turn it. But when I rattled the door in its frame, there was a metallic click, and the door swung open with a squeak of iron hinges, and a waft of dry, dusty air blew past me.

I could discern nothing of the interior, for it was pitch black beyond the door. The room either had no windows at all, or else they were covered over to admit no light. No matter how hard I peered within, I could not make out the contents, so I retrieved a candle from the library mantel and lit it from the gas flame on the wall. Thus prepared, I moved back to the door and stepped within.

The light of a single candle is an unsteady, flickering thing, but even the steady glow of gaslight would not have made the interior of the room seem less macabre.

Approximately twenty or so feet on each side, the space was a veritable shrine to death, containing as it did the preserved heads, skins, and whole bodies of more animals than I could count. I had seen hunters' trophy rooms before, but they consisted of a few choice examples to illustrate the owner's skill with a gun and boast of the exotic lands to which he had traveled. This, however, was either a collection of many generations or demonstrated a fixation bordering on the bizarre.

Fascinated, I picked out the animals I recognized: a grizzly bear, paw upraised and mouth open in a roar of defiance; a zebra skin stretched out on a frame and mounted to the wall like a painting; heads of moose and elk and deer, glass eyes staring back at me unblinkingly. There were more exotic animals as well, ones that must be from creatures I had read about but never seen. Surely the clawed creature with a beaver's tail and a duck's bill had to be a platypus from Australia, and I suspected the thing that looked like a cross between a zebra and a giraffe was an opaki from Africa. Other creatures I could not fathom at all; even the small brass plates on their stands displaying their Latin names offered me little insight. No doubt this was a naturalist's treasure trove. But while it would not have been out of place in a museum somewhere, stored away in a small, dark room in a private home like this, it seemed gruesome, perhaps even ghoulish.

I shivered, a chill running down my spine, and I turned to leave this place of death. But as I neared the door, I spotted something out of place pushed against the wall: a wooden chest, almost six feet long and about two feet wide and high. It was the only piece of furniture in the room, and I moved toward it, curious as to what it contained. I lifted the top and pushed it back, and I gaped at the contents in mystified disbelief.

While I was quite certain that, like Horatio, I was not aware of all things in heaven and earth, I was well acquainted with many of the myths and legends which seemed to be cultural archetypes, present in most human cultures. If my eyes did not deceive me, one such myth lay within the chest, a creature that could not possibly exist and yet somehow did.

Unlike the preserved multitude of animals in the room, this form had not been given over to the taxidermist's art. Instead, the corpse was dried and desiccated, the flesh shrunken on the bones until it resembled leather more than skin. The tail of the creature was long with one continuous fin running along the sides, like that of an eel. But it was the torso which caused me to gasp, for the flesh of the tail widened and expanded into a ribcage, rounding into shoulders that tapered into jointed arms, then split into five fingers, a delicate webbing still visible between them. Surmounting the shoulders was a head, strong-jawed and slit-mouthed, with round eye sockets above and small buds that must have been ears on the sides. Atop the head was the most disturbing thing of all: hair. Unmistakably hair and not fur, and although it was matted, it was quite long, and of a luxurious black, giving back a greenish tint in the light like the sheen of a raven's feather. It was not a human, nor a fish, but somehow a fusion of the two, the reality of it borne out by the brass plaque mounted on the edge of the chest.

Homo Piscine.

Certainly not the mermaid of legend, but so close I

had no doubt this must be one of the actual creatures that gave rise to the myths. Yet it could not exist! I was unable to believe the evidence before my eyes, certain it must be a hoax. For how could this creature exist in defiance of science and logic and even the teachings of religion? I could not tear my eyes away, fascinated and repulsed in equal measure. How had the creature gotten here? Where had it come from, and why had Roderick kept it a secret all these years?

I leaned in closer, noting the creature must have been female, for on closer examination the chest was topped with now-empty sacs that must once have been breasts. I could see now, too, the bullet hole on the sternum, a fatal wound for any humanoid creature. She had been shot, not hooked or harpooned or washed up on the shore. Shot by a hunter, who must have realized he was killing not only a unique creature but possibly an intelligent one as well.

As I was looking at her fine, dark hair, I noticed a rectangular object beside her head, which closer inspection revealed to be a leather-bound book. Loathe as I was to reach into the coffin—for coffin this most assuredly was—I was overwhelmed with a need to know what tome Roderick would have interred with this body. With a grimace, I snatched the book from its resting place, then backed away, and I found a place to rest the candlestick on the back of a stuffed mountain goat.

The book was old, the pages brittle with age and dryness, and I opened it with great care and delicacy. The first page declared in bold, black handwriting that it was the hunting journal of Roderick Anthony Heatherford, and my heart pounded as I turned the pages as quickly as I could without tearing them.

The journal began in 1836, the year Roderick turned twenty-one and attained his majority and his inheritance. He was quite a facile artist, for he included sketches of the animals he hunted, along with dates and places where he'd shot them. I sensed the mermaid had not come from India or Africa, or even Australia with its bizarre flora and fauna, so I kept searching until I found entries dated in September of 1849.

September the twenty-first: Tonight I was out later than usual, unable to sleep for the anticipation of my upcoming trip to Madagascar. I went for a walk by the river to tire myself, the path lit brilliantly by the light of the full moon. The river was quite calm, flowing wide and peaceful, and this, I am certain, is why I noticed the splashing. Looking out over the water, I saw them for the first time.

At first, I thought it was a group of people swimming, for I noticed heads and arms. Could it be escaped slaves, using the river to flee to freedom? But why would they be swimming upriver, against the current, in defiance of all sense? That was when I saw a form literally leap from the water, arcing up in the moonlight with a grace and power like that of a dolphin. But this was no dolphin, if such could even survive in the waters of the Pamlico. This was a form out of dreams and visions, out of the tales of sailors and seamen from the dawn of time. Part man, part some creature of the sea, it could not exist, and yet it did!

Entranced, I watched them, running along the riverbank to keep pace as they continued upstream. I could not accurately assess their number, but I would guess there were between thirty and forty of them, and I followed as far as I could, until the terrain was no longer passable. Then I stood for hours, staring out across the river, hoping they would come back, or more like them would happen along. But dawn arrived and I had seen no more, so I returned home.

I stopped reading and glanced back at the chest. So Roderick had seen the creatures right here on the river! But why had no one ever seen them before? I recalled no legends of creatures located anywhere other than at sea. I needed to know more, and I returned my attention to the journal.

For the next week, Roderick watched every night for the swimmers, certain they must return. He postulated if they came from the sea, perhaps, like salmon, they came upstream into the sheltered rivers to have their young. Which meant they would have to depart again, and he intended to be there when they did.

The entry for the first of October made my blood run cold.

October the first: I was right! My patience has been rewarded, for the swimmers have returned, this time headed down the river toward the ocean. I was waiting on the river-bank, and I saw them at last, although it was far more diffi-cult with the waning moon to see them in the darkness. But they came at last, and I waited, watching along the barrel of my gun, hands steady and sure as I held my breath. Then I saw one separate from the others, swimming closer to shore, possibly pursuing a fish. This was my chance! I let it approach, closer and closer, waiting for the moment when it would jump from the water, as they seemed wont to do. I knew I would get but one shot, and when the time came, I took it. A perfect hit, striking the creature in the middle of its chest! There was a shriek, the like of which I had never heard before, and I rushed forward, wading into the shallows, grabbing the body by its hair and pulling it to shore. I had my prize, a prize like no other! I was the first hunter to ever shoot a being out of legend!

My stomach clenched. I could not believe Roderick was celebrating killing this being, as though a creature so special, so unique, was of no more value than a bear or a fox. The arrogance of it angered me, as well as the callous way Roderick had lain in wait. He had done nothing to discover if these beings were closer to men than simple appearance; he cared not if they had souls as did those of us on land. All Roderick cared for was killing. Life meant nothing to him save in the ending of it.

I was about to slam the book closed and toss it away, when I saw the handwriting changed near the bottom of the page. It was still Roderick's, but it had lost its boldness, becoming cramped and shaky, as though the writer had suffered some injury or was under strain. I looked closer and saw the date was ten years after the entry where Roderick documented the killing of the creature.

1859, October the second: This has been a time of nightmares, but by some miracle I have survived it. The creatures I saw on the river ten years ago have lately returned. It was different this time, for I could hear them, their voices, sad and angry, calling to me, singing a song meant, I have no doubt, to lure me to them and thereby to my death. I know what they want: vengeance for the one I killed. They are sirens, these creatures, and their voices weave a spell for those they seek. But they shall not have me! When I heard them sing, I locked myself in my room and told O'Brien not to let me out for any reason, although he thought I was mad, for he does not hear the voices. Then I played the piano, drowning out their voices when they began to sing. That kept me from going to them, but alas, it did not save my nephew Philip. He arrived yesterday morning to pay me a visit, and he must have heard the voices, for he left the house and my cook saw him walk out into the river. He must have drowned, but his body has not yet been found. I am sorry for his death, but it was unavoidable, and it did cause the singers to leave. I yet live, and that is the important thing.

There it was, the reason for Garland's sleepwalking and for the tune he hummed incessantly. He heard the singers, too! I flipped through the last few journal entries, one each decade, wherein Roderick described the deaths of his relations. Such villainy turned my stomach, for after Philip's death, Roderick grew to believe he could save his own miserable life by sacrificing his male relations to the singers. It was pure cowardice, for he seemed convinced if he did not give the river singers a sacrifice, they would come up to the house to take him. For fifty years, he'd avoided his fate, and this year, he intended to sacrifice Garland.

I could not allow it, and I would not. This treachery would end now, for Roderick deserved whatever fate awaited him at the hands of the creatures he had wronged. I would not allow him to harm Garland or anyone else ever again.

I had to be subtle, and I hoped Roderick wouldn't attempt to prevent our leaving. However, I assumed Roderick would be less likely to do anything overt with Banning as a witness, since I could not imagine Roderick would want anyone to know about his acts of indirect murder. I would have preferred a person who was not connected to Roderick's interests, but this was a case of beggars being unable to be choosers.

I slipped the book into my pocket and retreated from the room, although I did not bother to close the door behind me. Let Roderick discover I knew his secret; I did not care, and perhaps it would serve as a warning his sins were not hidden in the darkness any longer.

I returned to Roderick's door and began to pace, checking my watch as I fretted over the amount of time that had passed. Afternoon was giving way to evening, and I debated knocking on the door and demanding Garland be released. But I waited, not wanting to prejudice Banning against me or worse, alarm Garland and have him doubt my sanity, given he knew nothing of what I had discovered.

It was almost six o'clock before the door finally opened, and I rushed forward as soon as I saw Garland. He exited alone and closed the door on the loud music which issued forth in his wake. I was relieved to have a moment to speak to him without being overheard.

"I've already packed for us. If you're ready, we can leave at once."

"I do not know of any reason why we cannot depart," Garland said. "Are you certain you do not wish to wait until morning, however? It will be dark soon, and it does not appear the storm has much abated."

"No, we must go!" I took Garland by the arm, leaning close and lowering my voice, although I found it hard to retain a calm demeanor. "There are things you do not know of. Horrible things. We must get away from this place tonight, even if we must walk."

Garland gaped at me, his eyes growing wide. "Geoffrey, do calm yourself! You are making no sense."

I glanced around, but we were still alone. "I cannot explain it all right now. There isn't time. But you must listen to me. You're in more danger than you know. I learned what happened to the other heirs. They—"

I broke off abruptly as the door opened once more, and Banning stepped out, carrying his case.

"Well, the business part of the day is finished." He seemed quite jovial, almost too much so. "Roderick has invited me to stay the night, given the storm. Seems like a good idea, don't you think, Garland? We can be away in the morning, when the storm will hopefully have blown itself out."

It was as though a lead weight dropped in my stomach, and I looked at Garland, pleading with my eyes. "Perhaps we can borrow your coach, and have it return for you tomorrow," I said, moving my gaze to Banning. "I'd prefer to go tonight."

Garland moved toward the window, his eyes growing glassy and distant. "I want to remain here," he said, his voice soft and dream-like, and he cocked his head as if listening for something. "The storm, you know. This house is strong and safe, not nearly as awful as I first thought."

I stared at Garland in dismay, cursing myself for not barging into Roderick's room earlier and removing Garland by force. Some aspect of the song must be affecting him, even though he was awake.

"No! We have to go." I glanced at Banning, then moved to Garland's side, taking him by the shoulders and turning him around, forcing him to look at me. I gazed into his eyes, which seemed to be glazing over as I watched. I shook him. "Please, Garland, we need to leave."

Garland frowned as he struggled to focus on my face,

and it seemed the fog began to clear from his eyes. "Yes… Yes, we should leave right away…."

"Now see here, Mr. Wainwright!" Banning stepped up beside me, and I whirled to face him. "You're acting very odd. Mr. Heatherford wishes to remain, and I believe it would be insanity to head out in this storm. Since the coach is mine, and I am remaining, you have no choice but to stay the night."

I was becoming desperate, and I thought of the gun in my pocket. If necessary, I could commandeer both Garland and the coach and leave Banning behind. They would think me quite mad, but I didn't care; all that mattered was getting Garland away.

I began to move my hand toward my coat pocket. "Staying is not an option," I said harshly. "You don't know what's going on here! We have to leave because—"

"Behind you!" Garland shouted, his gaze frantic as it fixed on something over my shoulder.

I reached for the gun and spun around, but I was far too late. Time slowed down as my horrified eyes saw O'Brien rushing toward me, arms upraised and a fireplace poker clutched in his hands. Before I could do more than open my mouth to shout, the poker descended toward me. There was a flash of pain greater than anything I had ever known, and my vision dimmed as I lost control of my body. I could feel myself falling, and I had a brief moment of agony as I realized I had failed to protect Garland. Then my body hit the floor, darkness stole over me, and I knew no more.

CHAPTER 6

Beethoven's 9th symphony, *Ode to Joy*, flowed over and around me and through me, and I wondered how anything so beautiful could hurt so much. My head throbbed, and I moaned as I attempted to lift my hands to my ears to protect them from the relentless crescendo of the music.

My body was overcome by languorous weight, and my arms responded slowly to the commands of my brain as I strived to lift one hand to my head. My fingers encountered something damp and sticky, matting my hair, and I returned to awareness. Somehow I was still alive.

I opened my eyes and blinked at the brightness as I tried to focus on my surroundings. I was lying on a carpet, and a few feet away, I could see wheels. I winced at the pain of rolling my head, but then I could make out the form of Roderick, sitting in his wheelchair. The old man looked haggard, as though he hadn't slept in days, and terrified as well. The very expression on his face gave me hope, for if he wasn't gloating at his success, perhaps Garland yet lived.

Garland needs me. I have to save him. The words were a mantra in my mind as I forced my body to do my bidding. I had to get to my feet, and no labor of Hercules had ever seemed as impossible as the simple act of raising my head from the floor.

Pain lanced through me, and I gritted my teeth against it, thinking only of the man I loved as I struggled upright. Bitter bile rose in my throat, but I swallowed it down. I did not have the time to be weak. Every moment I delayed was a moment of Garland's life ticking away.

Alerted by my movement, Roderick turned his malevolent gaze on me. "You yet live? Well, no matter. O'Brien will see to you later."

"Not if I see to him first," I retorted, although the words were slurred, my tongue feeling thick and heavy. There was a table beside me, and I gripped one leg and used it to pull myself upright. My head was pounding and my stomach roiled, but I was not going to give up.

"No!" Roderick's voice was tinged with desperation. "You must not leave this room. Stay, and I will grant you anything it is in my power to give. Wealth beyond your imagining can be yours!"

I was almost on my feet, although my knees trembled with the effort. Roderick would have been furious to realize his words, rather than tempting me, only strengthened my will to fight. To put a price on a life, to offer to pay me to be an accomplice to his decades of evil, only gave fuel to my determination.

"All I want is Garland," I growled, glaring at him with all the anger and disgust I felt. "To me, he is beyond price."

That was not the answer Roderick wanted, and his weathered face contorted in a snarl as he wheeled himself over to the hearth and snatched up a poker, which he brandished at me. "Then you may join him in hell!"

Standing at last, I rested both hands on the table and waited for the room to stop swimming. "Hell is your destination, not his."

I didn't bother to watch Roderick's reaction. I was looking at the table, on which sat the gramophone blaring the strains of Beethoven. Roderick was using it to drown out the voices of the singers, so he didn't have to hear the melody summoning him to his fate. I bared my teeth as I swung my fist and knocked the player off the table. There was a horrible shriek as the needle skidded across the cylinder, and then it crashed to the floor, and the music stopped.

Roderick dropped the poker and clapped his hands over his ears. "What have you done?"

I straightened and snarled at the old man. "What should have been done years ago."

With that, I made my unsteady way to the door with as much speed as I could manage. Roderick cried out again, a mournful wail wrenched from a soul mired in horror, and he tried to follow. His pursuit was short-lived, however, and he stopped and covered his ears again as he slumped helplessly in his wheelchair.

I didn't care what happened to Roderick, who deserved no sympathy in the face of his sins. I reached the door and turned the knob, dismayed to find it locked from the outside.

I rattled the door, panic rising up as my own horror threatened to overcome me. But then I recalled the gun in my pocket, and I fumbled uselessly before pulling it forth at last. I had to brace it with both hands, but I cocked it, aimed at the lock, and squeezed the trigger.

The gun kicked in my hands, and I was deafened by the sound, but the entire doorknob disintegrated, and the door snapped back on its hinges. Without a backward glance, I staggered out into the hallway, desperate to find Garland. I knew where I had to go, because there was only one place O'Brien would take him.

As I made my way toward the kitchen, I became aware something seemed odd, but it wasn't until I wrenched open the kitchen door that I realized what it was. The storm had abated; there was no rain, no close thunder or lightning, and the wind had given way to a dead calm.

Surprised, I peered out warily, on guard lest O'Brien or Banning or some other accomplice was guarding against interference. But there was no one in evidence, and I made my way down the steps and walked across the lawn, my shoes growing wet and stained by the remnants of the river muck.

The moon was above the tree line, full and bloated and as malevolent as everything else about this accursed place. But it provided enough light for me to see, and I grimaced as I stepped past the skeleton which sprawled grotesquely as though trying to make its way to the house. I could hear distant thunder, but there came the closer sound of rushing water, and above it rose the eerie, plaintive sound of voices, crooning out a melody in which heartbreak and vengeance were mixed in equal measure. I recognized the song at once from the snatches Garland had hummed, and the hair on the back of my neck rose as I knew with utter certainty I heard the singers of the river, the kin of the poor, murdered female who lay among Roderick's trophies.

I quickened my pace, my own pain forgotten as I caught sight of someone standing on a small dock at the river's edge. Although he faced away from me, I knew without a doubt it was Garland, from the slender elegance of his form and the way the moonlight shone on his golden hair, bleaching it to silver. I staggered forward and slipped in the muck, hoping he was not so enthralled by the singing that he could not hear me.

"Garland! Don't go into the water! I beg you! Listen to me!"

But Garland didn't so much as glance back, and he stretched out his arms as if welcoming his fate.

"Get away from here!" O'Brien's snarling voice distracted me from Garland, and I spun to see him stationed on the bank of the river, well away from the water but positioned to block my way to the dock.

"You can go to hell with your master!" I shouted, as O'Brien ran toward me. I lifted the gun and fired.

I heard him shriek in pain, but he didn't fall. Before I could fire again, he was on me, and I skidded in the mud and dropped the gun, and I went down hard with O'Brien on top of me.

The man was strong despite his age, and I struggled to free myself as he tried to get his hands around my throat. I grabbed his wrist, and then I wrapped my legs around his hips. I used all my strength to roll us to one side, and surprise bloomed in his eyes when he found himself beneath me with one of his arms now pinned behind him.

I drew in a breath and shouted as loudly as I could.

"Garland! Garland, listen to me! It's Geoff! Don't leave me!"

I spared a glance at the dock, where Garland still stood, bathed in moonlight, arms raised like some sacrifice to a primitive god, and my heart thudded painfully. O'Brien used my distraction to deliver a vicious punch to my jaw, and my head rang with the force of the blow. I lost my grip on his wrist, falling to one side with a grunt, and the older man wasted no time in once again getting the upper hand. He punched me again and again, and I flung out my arm, trying to reach the gun or a rock I could use to beat off the attack. My hand encountered something hard and round, and I didn't stop to think, for O'Brien's hands were around my throat. I bashed O'Brien in the head with the object. He grunted, but his hands kept squeezing. I desperately hit him again and again, beating him with all my strength as spots danced in my vision. A fourth blow and a fifth, and the pressure on my throat suddenly slackened. I hit him once more, and he slid off me, falling to the side in a boneless heap.

It took a moment for me to get air back into my lungs and for my vision to lose the tinge of red it had developed. I rolled and pushed O'Brien's legs off of mine, and then I struggled upright. I looked down at O'Brien, whose forehead was bloody and misshapen. I spared a glance at the object in my hand, and then I dropped it with a gasp of horror.

I had beaten O'Brien to death with a human skull.

The night had descended into total madness, but I could not forget my purpose. The voices were still singing, and I staggered forward toward the dock.

"Garland! Garland!"

My injuries hindered me, and I tripped and fell, noting with eerie detachment I had stumbled over yet another skeleton, this one with flesh and hair still clinging to the skull. I could not rise to my feet; the fall had twisted my leg and the best I could do was to crawl forward. Still I cried out to Garland, begging him not to leave me and imploring him to ignore the singers.

At last, Garland lowered his arms, and he glanced around, appearing dazed and bewildered. When his gaze fell on me, he seemed to shake off the effect of the singing at the sight of me lying broken and bloody on the ground.

"Geoffrey!"

He sounded so much like his old self that I could have wept, and he ran toward me. Before he could make it off the dock, however, a form staggered out of the shadows, and I shouted out a warning when I recognized Roderick tottering on unsteady legs as though the act of walking was agony. Garland seemed transfixed by the shock of seeing Roderick on his feet, but only for a moment. He began moving toward me again, and Roderick veered to block his path.

Garland hesitated, seeming unwilling to engage the old man, but Roderick had no such qualms. As soon as he was in reach, he lunged at Garland, and I gleaned his intention was to herd Garland onto the dock and into the water. Garland backed up, his expression torn as he stared at Roderick, and I could only pray his sense of self-preservation overcame his reservations about harming a frail, elderly man. Roderick would not show him such mercy.

As they moved onto the dock, dozens of pale arms rose out of the water, reaching for a victim. I doubted they cared which man fell into their grasp. Garland continued to move backward until they were well away from the shore, and the singing grew louder and more frenetic. With a wild cry, Roderick lunged forward again —and Garland grabbed his withered arms and flung him over the side of the dock. The singing changed to a high, inhuman ululation of victory as Roderick tumbled into the waiting arms of the singers; he had no time to make a sound before they dragged him under, and not even bubbles followed in his wake.

Garland stood still, watching the spot where Roderick had been dragged under with an implacable gaze. I stared at him, surprised but fiercely proud of his resourcefulness in luring Roderick out onto the dock. I was grateful he had not hesitated to send the old man to the fate he so richly deserved. At last, he turned his back on the river and hurried to my side. When he reached me, I was relieved to see he was uninjured.

"I was trying to rescue you, but it seems you rescued yourself." I smiled wryly. "Perhaps next time, you may play the hero."

"I've no desire to be a hero. Or rather, I should prefer not to find myself in another situation that requires it." Garland stretched out his hand when he drew near, regarding me with concern. "Can you get up?"

I took his hand and let him help me to my feet, wincing in pain as my left leg took my weight. Fortunately, it was not broken, so I tugged Garland's hand and drew him closer so I could wrap my arms around him.

"I'm fine, especially now you are safe. When O'Brien knocked me out, I thought I had failed you."

Garland slid his arms around my waist in return and clung to me. "I cannot claim to understand any of this. All

I know is that my uncle meant to do me harm as he must have done to my predecessors. But why?"

I pulled back so I could look into Garland's troubled eyes. "I believe I've pieced together the tale."

I looked toward the river, where the singers were still crooning, although the tone of their song had changed. The vengeance was gone from the melody, which had now become one of satisfaction, yet also sadness and yearning. It touched a chord in me, for that is what I would have felt if Garland and I had been parted.

"I think I know how to end this, once and for all, but I'll need your help. We need to retrieve something from the house, and I'll tell you what I have learned."

We made our way through the mud, past O'Brien's still form and past the four bodies whose identities I now believed I knew: Garland's cousins, the ones who had died before him, sent back to land by the singers. I was not certain if they'd meant the gesture as an entreaty or a warning; perhaps it was both. I explained this to Garland and told him about his somnambulism, and about my theory his relatives had been lured by the singers as they attempted to summon Roderick. I related my experiences in Roderick's room, and then I led him to the small room where the body of the mermaid lay.

"I think they want her back," I said, clinging to Garland's hand as we regarded the contents of the chest. "Who knows how long fifty years is to them? They must still grieve for her and wished to avenge her murder. I think we should return her to her loved ones."

Garland's eyes filled with sorrow as my tale unfolded, and he bent to pick up the desiccated body and cradled it tenderly in his arms. "Yes, we should. Let us end their suffering and return her to the sea, where she belongs."

I limped along at Garland's side as he carried the body back outside. Roderick's wheelchair was on the porch where he'd left it. Perhaps the song from the river had lured him, or perhaps he wanted to make certain Garland died to appease the singers. Whatever the reason, the old man had met his fate at last with the sin of not just one, but five murders on his soul.

We reached the dock, and I remained close by Garland's side, although I realized this was his task to perform. Hopefully this act would end the cycle of death and give the souls of Roderick's victims peace.

Garland walked to the end of the dock, his demeanor as somber as any pallbearer, and he bore the creature's body with respectful dignity. When he reached the end, he knelt, not seeming to care about the wet muck coating his trousers.

"I'm sorry your loss. I'm sorry for what Roderick did to her," he said as lowered the body into the water.

The multitude of sickly pale arms reached out again, and I was terrified they would grab Garland and drag him down, but they embraced the body of their long-lost companion instead. I rested my hand on Garland's shoulder and squeezed it gently, as the singing voices grew louder and louder, a crescendo of sound that seemed to vibrate the very air around us. Then, in a single breath, the voices stopped, and the only sounds to reach our ears was the murmur of the river and the fading sound of distant thunder.

"I think it may be over," I said. "At last."

"May they rest in peace." Garland looked at the bodies on the shore and then back at the water. "All of them."

"Amen." My answer was fervent, and as Garland rose, I slid my arm around his waist. "I suppose we'll have to stay and deal with the others tomorrow. Is there any use in asking if Banning remained? I had hopes he might not be in your uncle's confidence and would be unwilling to condone murder."

"If he is not an accomplice, he is at least complicit," Garland said, his expression turning hard and grim. "I remember little of the last few hours, but I do remember seeing him depart in haste after you were hurt. No doubt he wanted to retain what little plausible deniability he could."

"To think Shakespeare had the measure of lawyers three hundred years ago." I gave Garland a squeeze. "Do you feel we could sleep here tonight safely? I don't believe I'm up for walking all the way to town, even if the rain has finally stopped."

Garland cast a dubious look at O'Brien's body where it lay sprawled on the mucky ground. "Is he dead or unconscious? My uncle is gone, and I doubt Banning will poke his nose through the door until he is summoned. He is our only remaining concern," he said, pointing to O'Brien.

I wrinkled my nose, but I released Garland and went to press my fingers against O'Brien's neck. His skin was cold, and I detected no pulse and no breath; up close, I could see I'd caved in his skull. Part of me felt remorse for having ended a life, but he had left me no choice. We had tried to walk away from this place, and O'Brien's choice to serve evil had been responsible for his death; I had been the instrument, nothing more.

"Yes, he is dead." I straightened. "If I hadn't killed him, he would have killed me, as Roderick would have killed you. I believe we can sleep with clear consciences tonight."

Garland breathed a deep sigh of relief. "Then I believe we will be safe here tonight. Tomorrow, we will see to the remains and find a credible lawyer so I may collect my inheritance. I have no intention of letting Banning see to my affairs."

I nodded in agreement, and we began walking slowly toward the house. As we approached, I looked up at it, and for the first time, it no longer appeared menacing, as though the lack of Roderick and his evil presence had somehow removed the shadows which had lurked over it. I thought perhaps being filled with love instead of darkness and death, it might one day become a home—maybe even *our* home. We had no reason to fear the singers any longer, and what man could resist the lure of knowing that some myths and legends were true, and he might be blessed to witness something truly magical? Since we had been touched by the arcane, I thought Garland and I might find ourselves seeing and hearing other things of a fantastic nature. Little did I know, in those moments of joy and relief, how prescient my feelings would be.

But those are other tales, for another time.

ABOUT THE AUTHOR

Rachel Langella and Ari McKay are the professional pseudonyms for Arionrhod and McKay, who have been writing together for over a decade. Their collaborations encompass a wide variety of romance genres, including contemporary, fantasy, science fiction, gothic, and action/adventure. Their work includes the Blood Bathory series of paranormal novels, the Herc's Mercs series, as well as two historical Westerns: *Heart of Stone* and *Finding Forgiveness*. When not writing, they can often be found scheming over costume designs or binge watching TV shows together.

Ari McKay is a retired systems engineer turned full-time writer and seamstress. Now that she is an empty-nester, she has turned her attentions to finding the perfect piece of land to build a fortress in preparation for the zombie apocalypse, and baking (and eating) far too many cakes.

Rachel Langella is a creative writing teacher who has been writing for one reason or another most of her life. She loves all things spooky and/or vintage, and she's given in to Ari's corruptive influences and learned to sew so she can make her own vintage-style clothes and costumes. Given she has the survival skills of a gnat, she's relying on Ari to help her survive the zombie apocalypse.

Visit Rachel and Ari on:
   Website: arimckay.com
   Facebook:
   https://www.facebook.com/ari.mckay.7
   And
   https://www.facebook.com/rachel.langella.9

Twitter:
   @AriMcKay1
   And
   @LangellaRachel

When Harlan is provoked into an unexpected transformation, Whimsy uses his magic to ease Harlan's pain, but with an unexpected consequence. While he's shifted, Harlan's wolf recognizes Whimsy as his mate.

Yet even as they try to figure out their relationship given Harlan's doubts, suspicious events in the Asheville magical community escalate. Shifters are disappearing, others are murdered, and Harlan's curse makes him an obvious target. It will take all of Whimsy's magic to drive back the rising evil—and if he fails, Harlan will lose not only his life, but his very soul.

Quenched In Blood

Vampire Julian Schaden warned the Asheville Paranormal Council of an impending demonic incursion for decades. Over the past two years, he and his friends have fought hard with little help because Micah Carter, the demon hunter who should have led them, abandoned his responsibilities long before his death.

In desperation, Julian visits the Carter property and finds a miracle: Thomas Carter, heir to a long line of demon hunters. Thomas knows nothing about the supernatural world, but the prospect of a real life outside the sheltered, isolated farm calls to him, and the idea of fighting the Unholy feels right.

Thomas is too young and innocent for Julian, but opposites attract, and this is one battle Julian seems fated to lose. But a prophecy from a dying mage comes with a bleak warning: the upcoming battle will claim Thomas's life. To keep the world safe, Julian may have to sacrifice the only love he's ever known.

www.ingramcontent.com/pod-product-compliance
Lightning Source LLC
Chambersburg PA
CBHW031431130726
47989CB00003B/1088